Putuguq & Kublu

AND THE ATTACK OF THE AMAUTALIK!

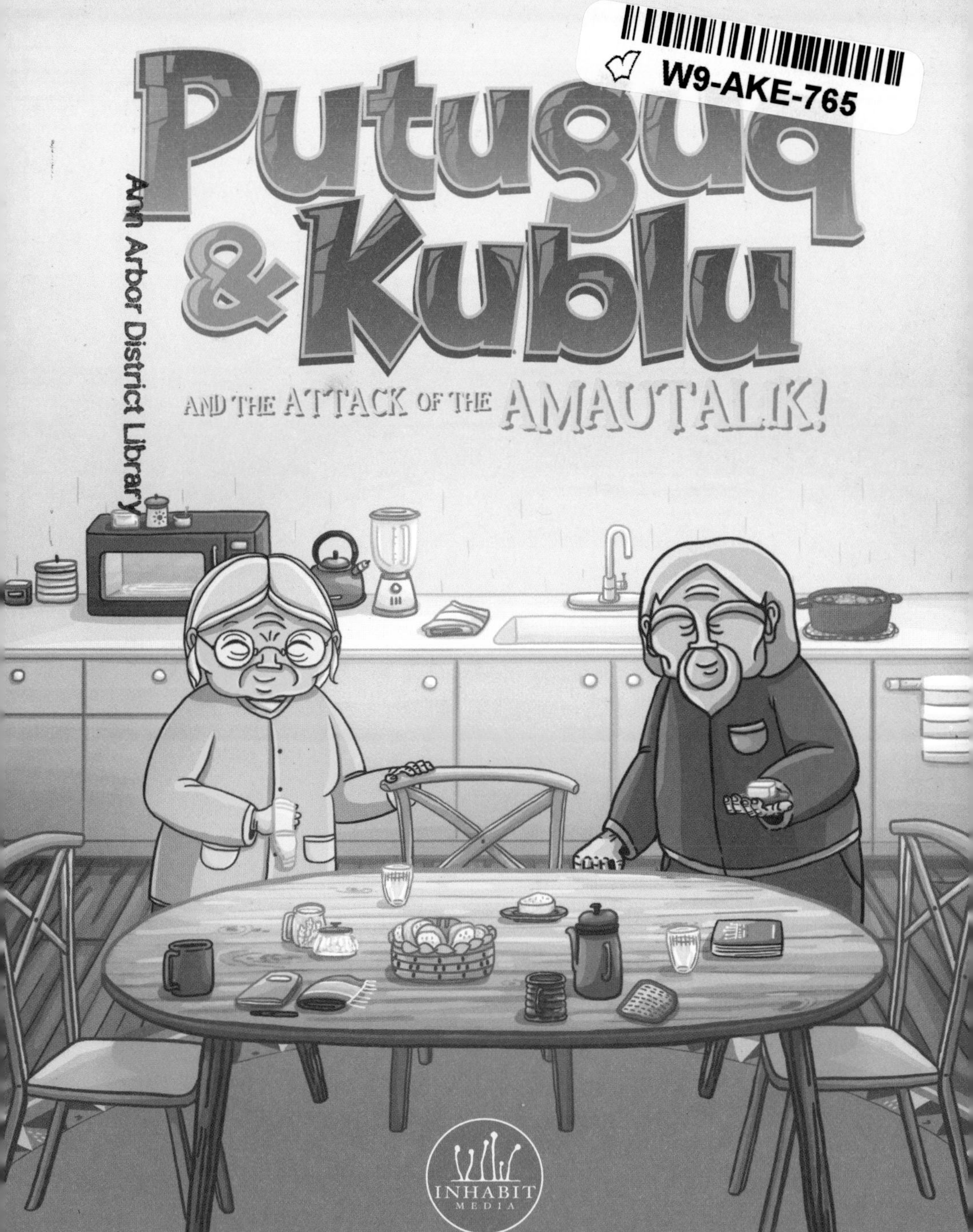

INHABIT MEDIA

Iqaluit • Toronto

Published by Inhabit Media Inc. | www.inhabitmedia.com

Inhabit Media Inc. (Iqaluit) P.O. Box 11125, Iqaluit, Nunavut, X0A 1H0

Design and layout copyright © 2022 Inhabit Media Inc.
Text copyright © 2022 Roselynn Akulukjuk and Danny Christopher
Illustrations by Astrid Arijanto copyright © 2022 Inhabit Media Inc.

Editors: Neil Christopher, Louise Flaherty, and Kelly Ward
Art director: Danny Christopher and Astrid Arijanto

We acknowledge the support of the Canada Council for the Arts for our
publishing program.

This project was made possible in part by the Government of Canada.

ISBN: 978-1-77227-419-6

Printed in Canada.

Library and Archives Canada Cataloguing in Publication

Title: Putuguq & Kublu and the attack of the amautalik! /
by Roselynn Akulukjuk and Danny Christopher ;
illustrated by Astrid Arijanto.
Other titles: Putuguq and Kublu and the attack of the amautalik!
Names: Akulukjuk, Roselynn, author. | Christopher, Danny, 1975- author. |
Arijanto, Astrid, illustrator.
Identifiers: Canadiana 20220156670 | ISBN 9781772274196 (softcover)
Subjects: LCGFT: Graphic novels. | LCGFT: Comics (Graphic works)
Classification: LCC PN6733.A37 P88 2022 | DDC j741.5/971—dc23

Putuguq & Kublu

AND THE ATTACK OF THE AMAUTALIK!

By Roselynn Akulukjuk and Danny Christopher
Illustrated by Astrid Arijanto

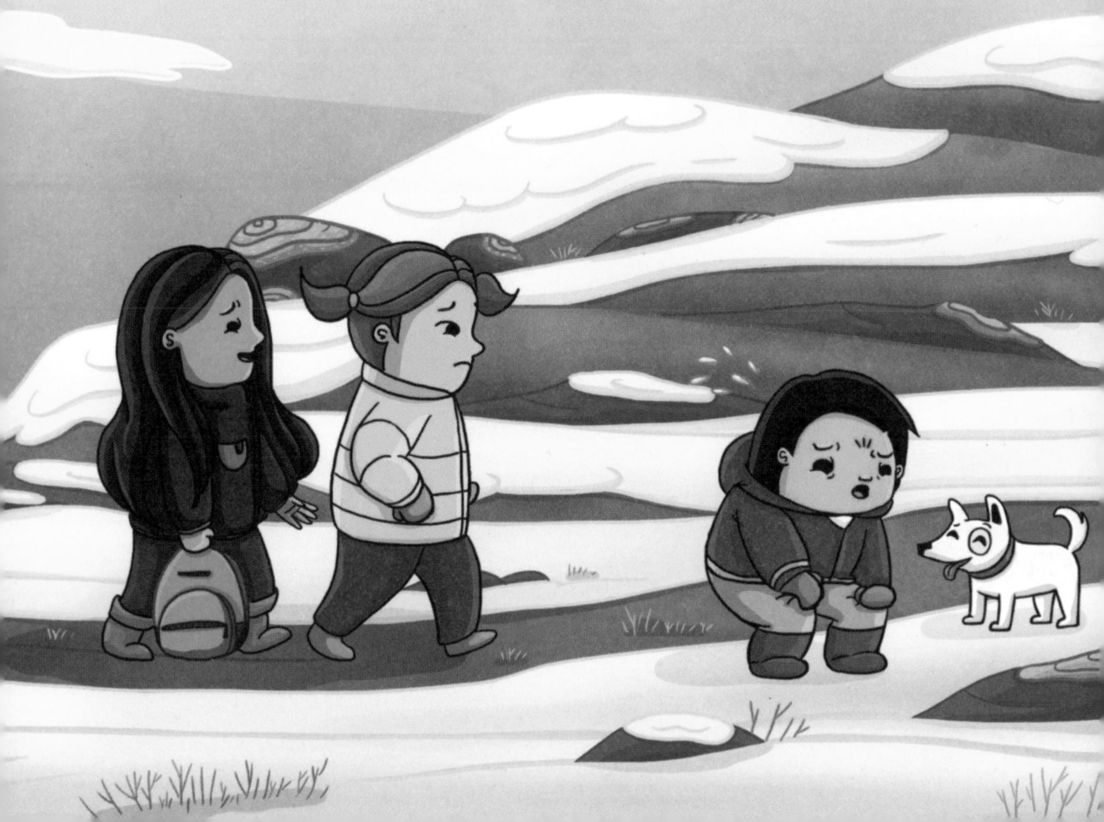

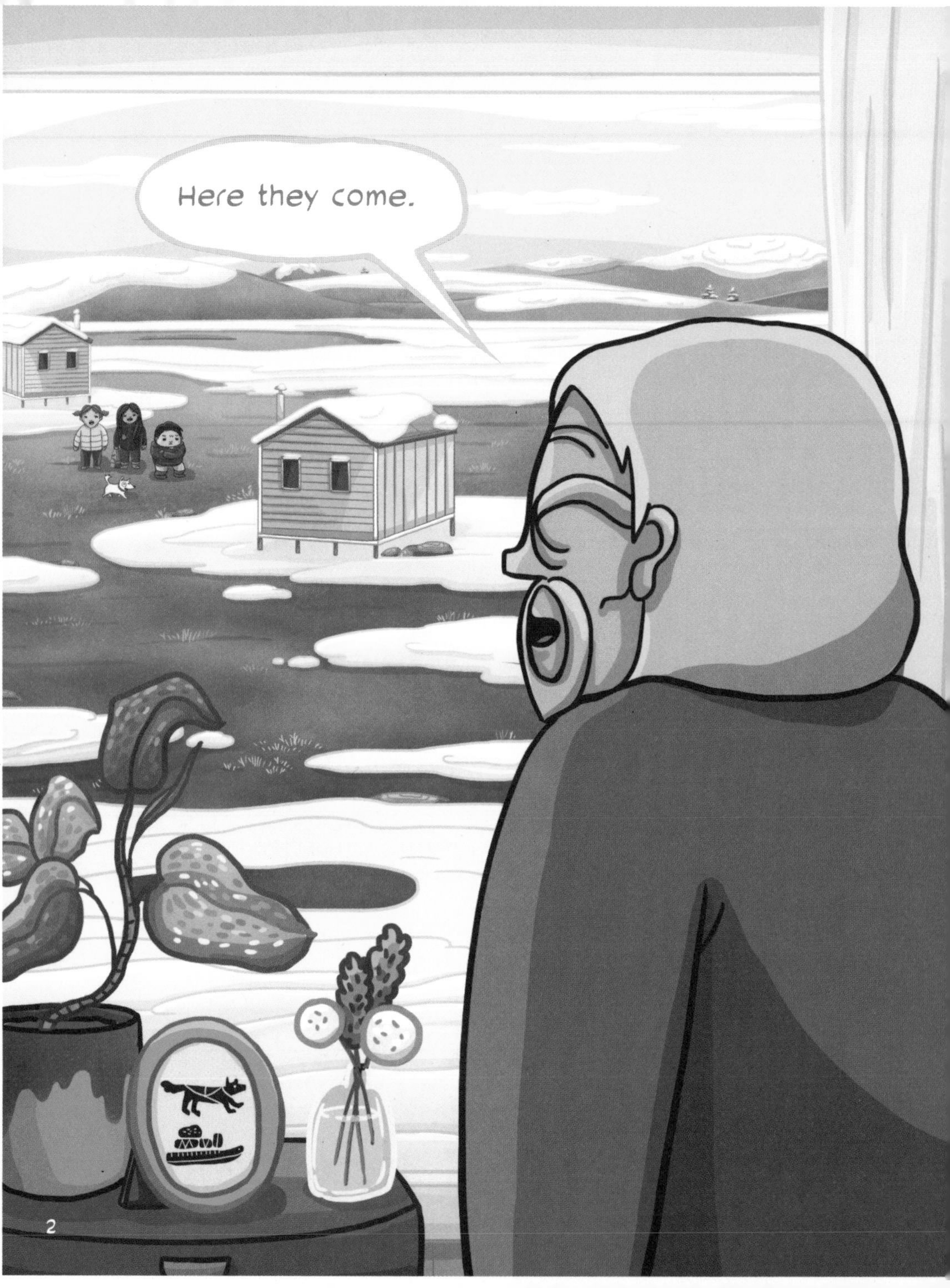
Here they come.

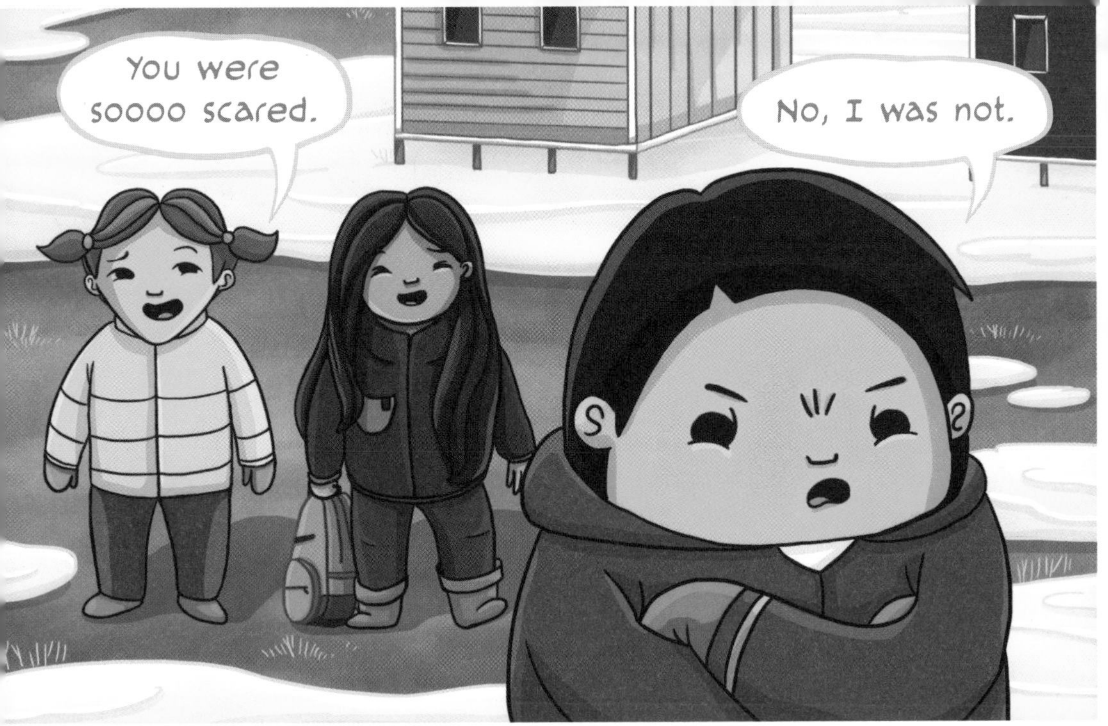
You were soooo scared.
No, I was not.

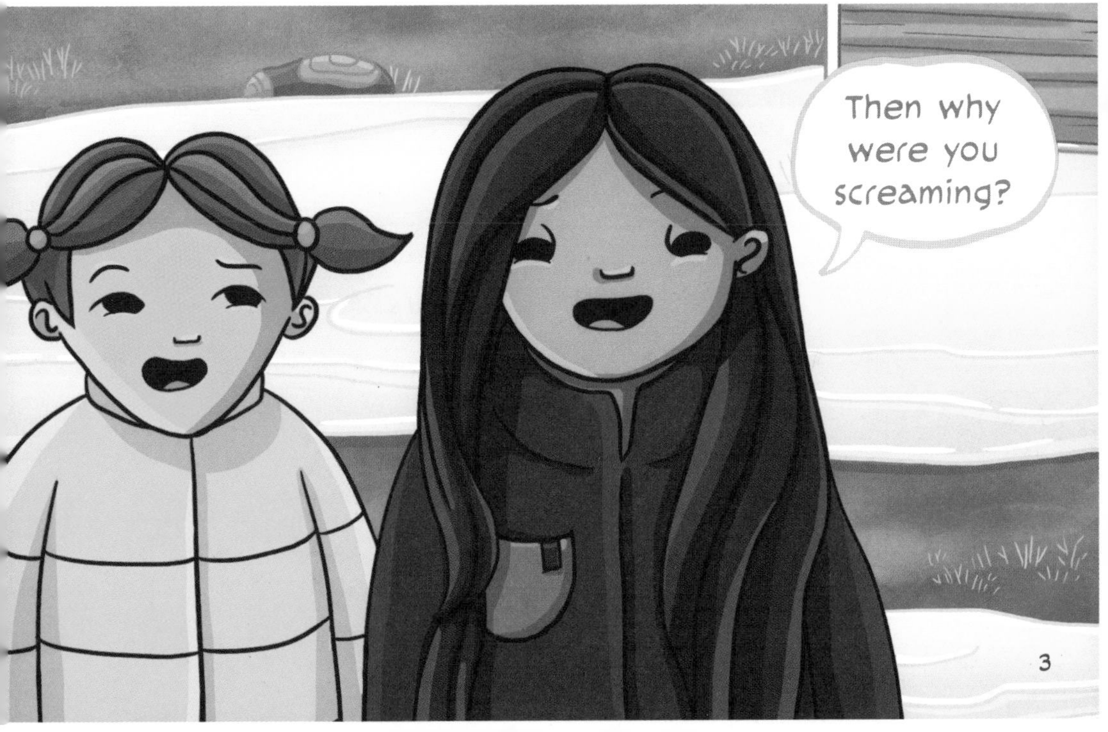
Then why were you screaming?

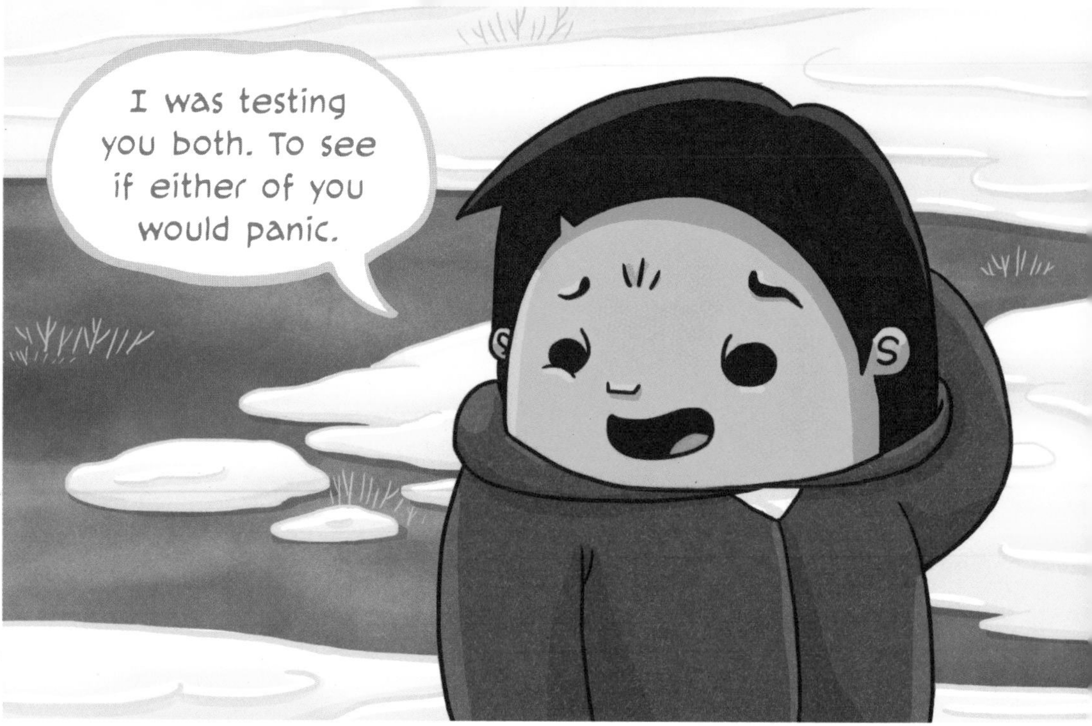
I was testing you both. To see if either of you would panic.

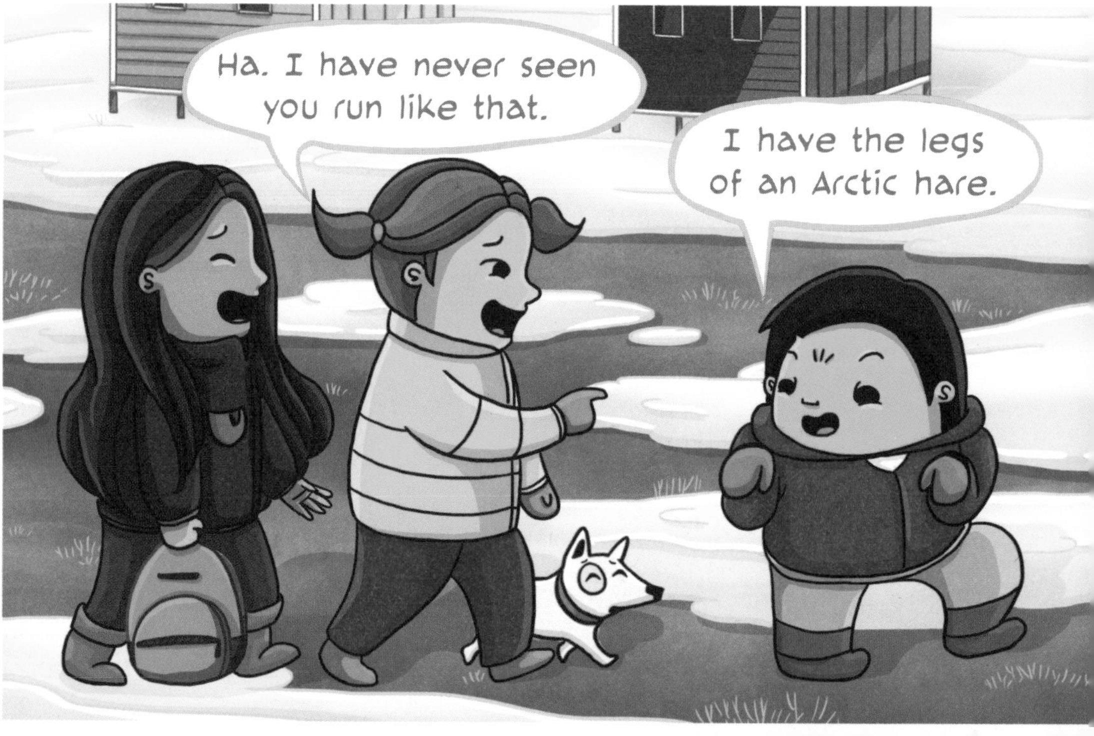
Ha. I have never seen you run like that.
I have the legs of an Arctic hare.

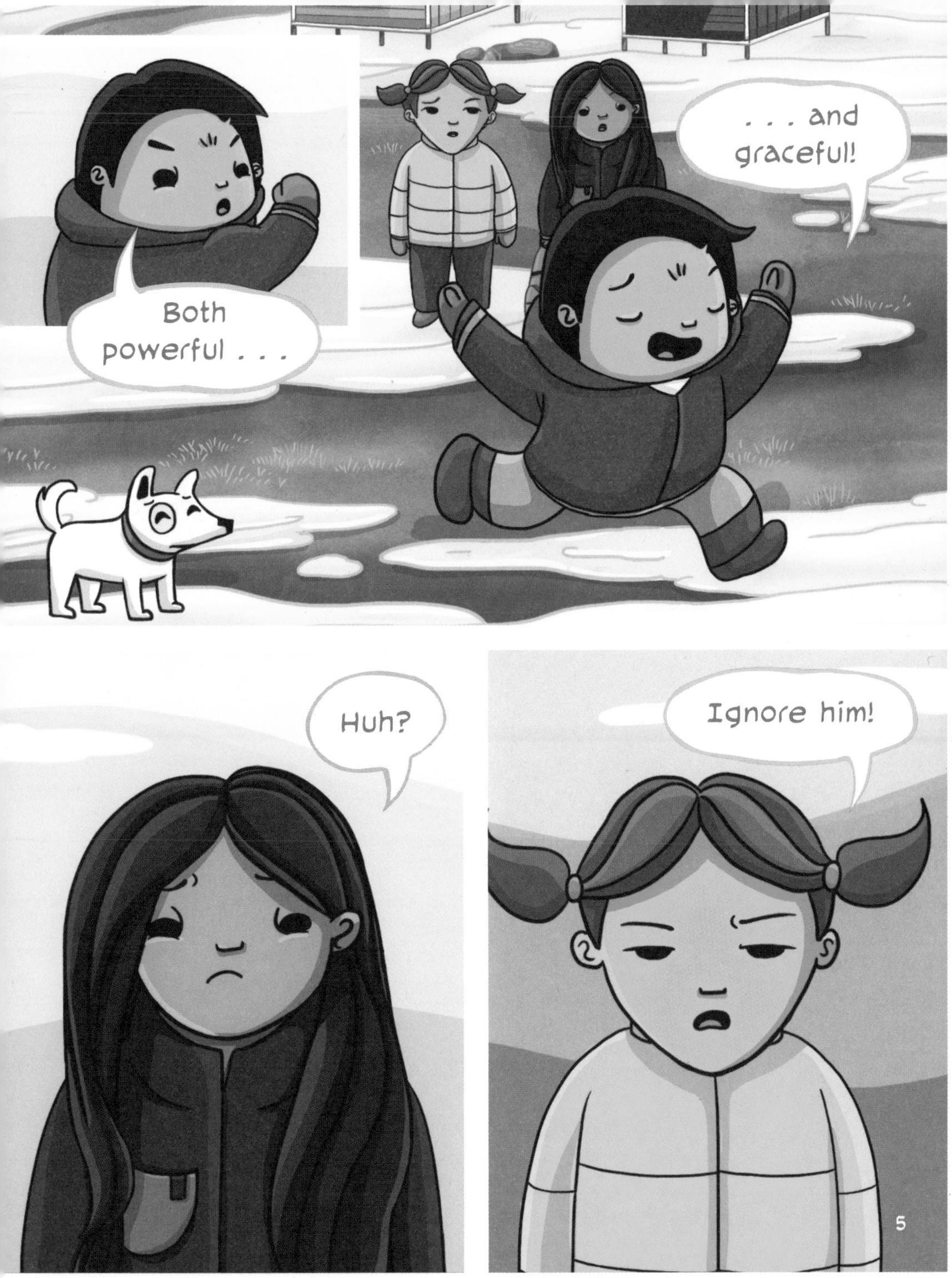
Both powerful . . .
. . . and graceful!
Huh?
Ignore him!

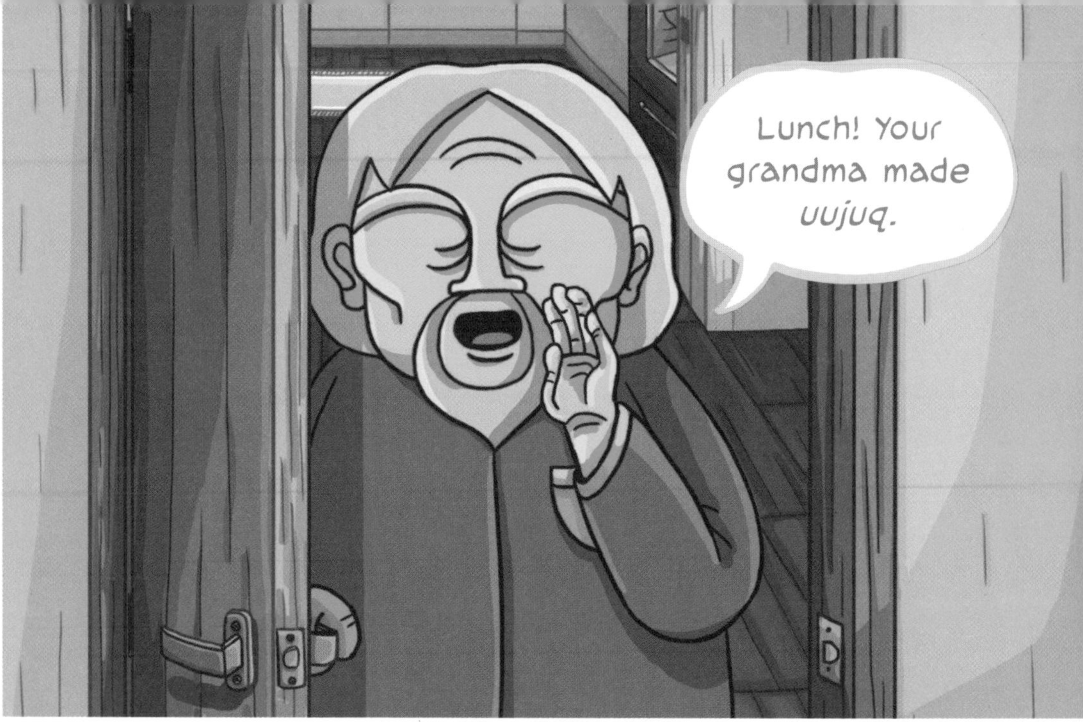
Lunch! Your grandma made *uujuq*.

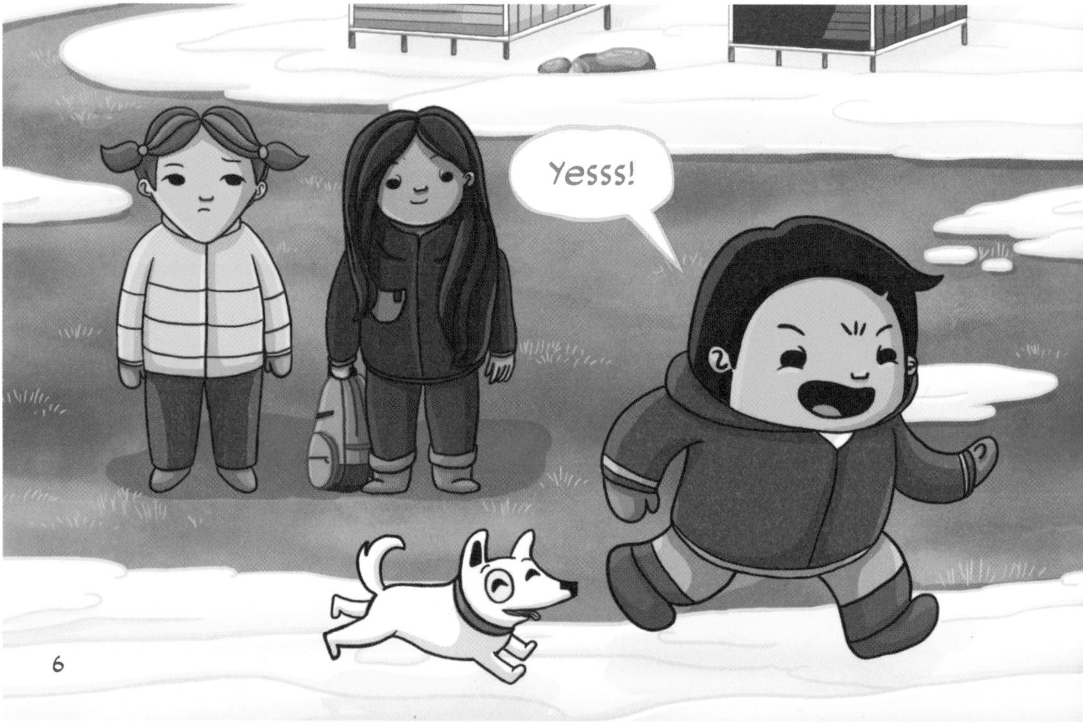
Yesss!

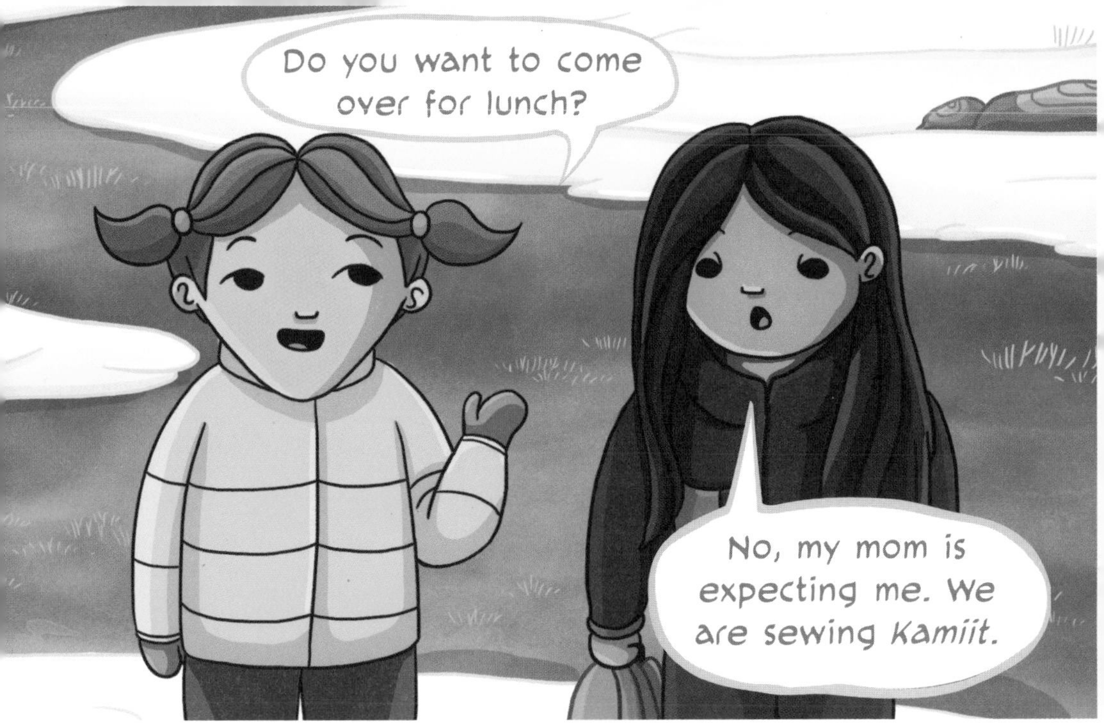
Do you want to come over for lunch?
No, my mom is expecting me. We are sewing *Kamiit*.

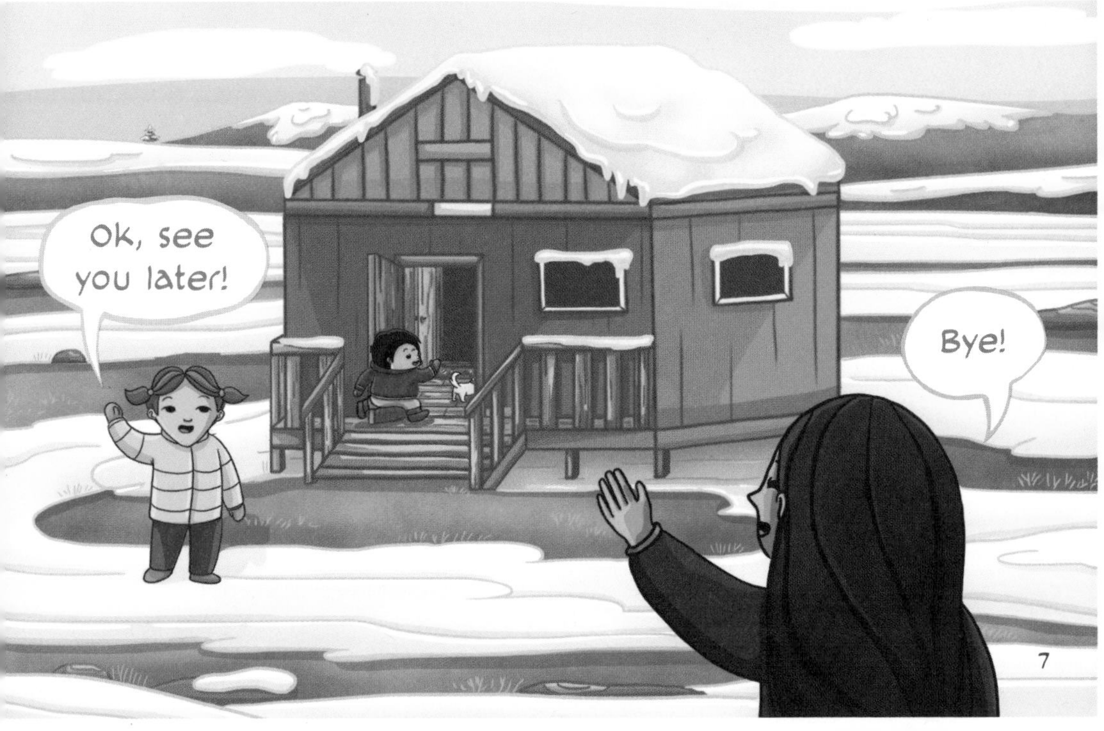
Ok, see you later!
Bye!

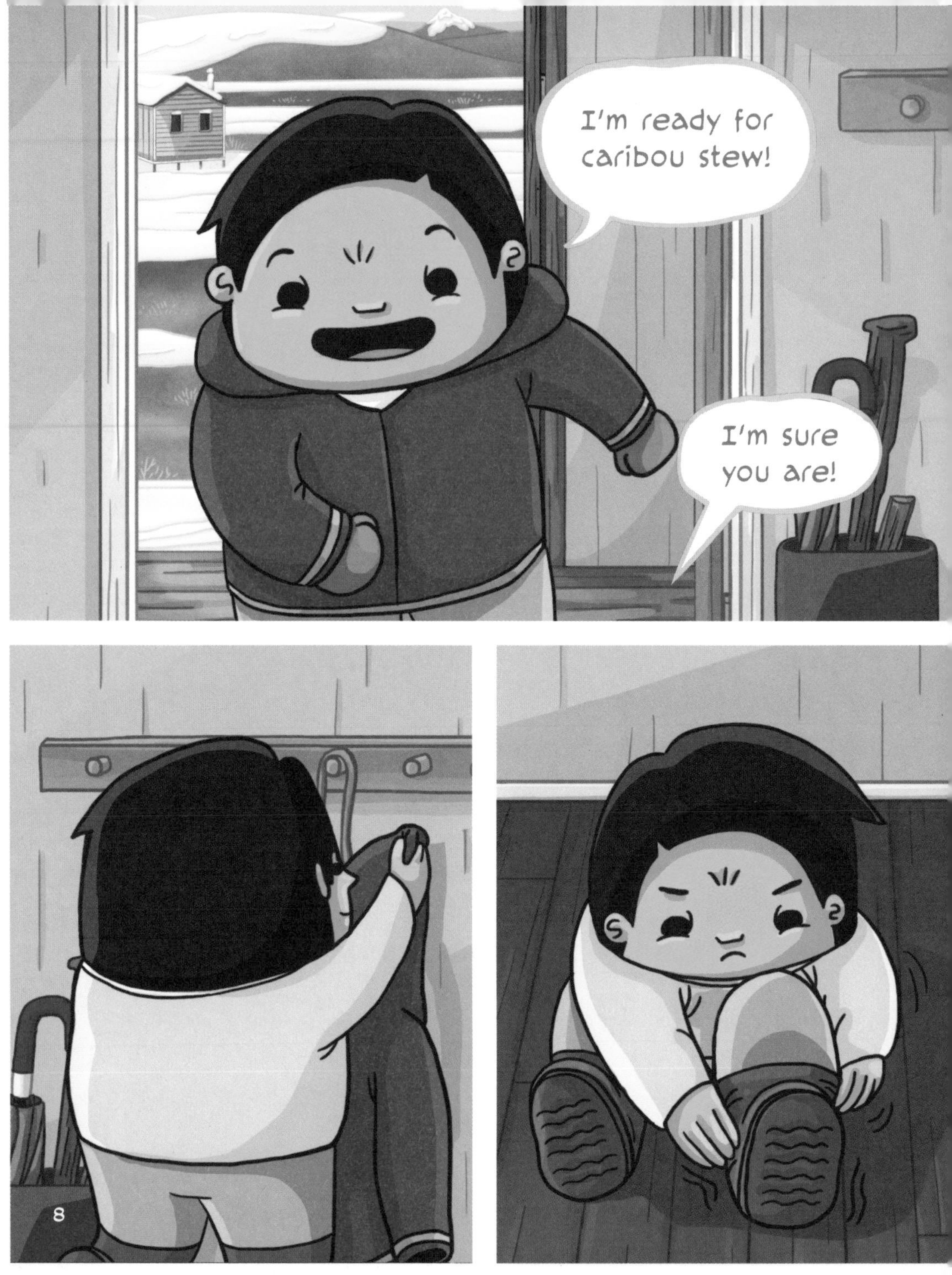
I'm ready for caribou stew!
I'm sure you are!

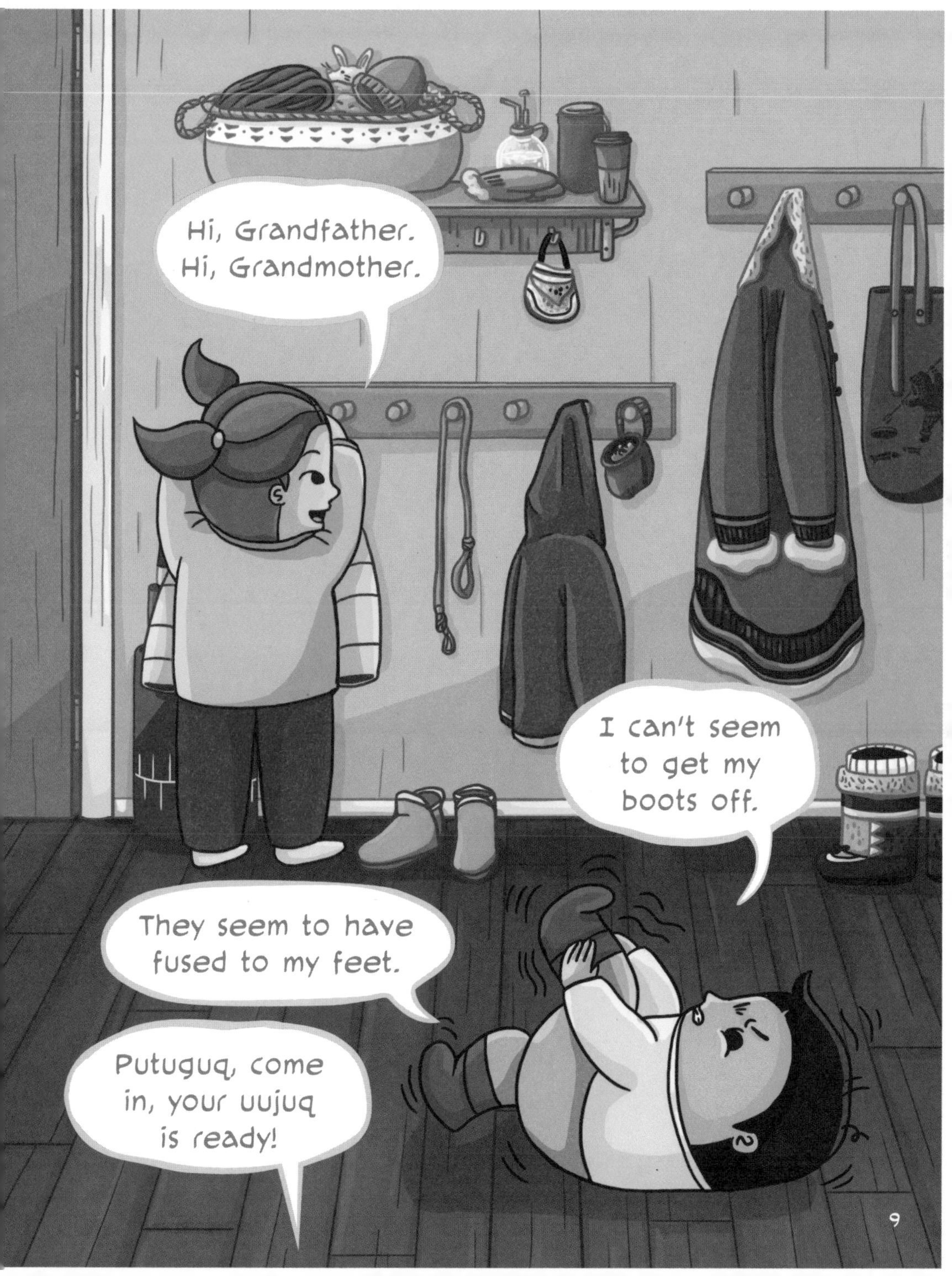
Hi, Grandfather. Hi, Grandmother.
I can't seem to get my boots off.
They seem to have fused to my feet.
Putuguq, come in, your uujuq is ready!

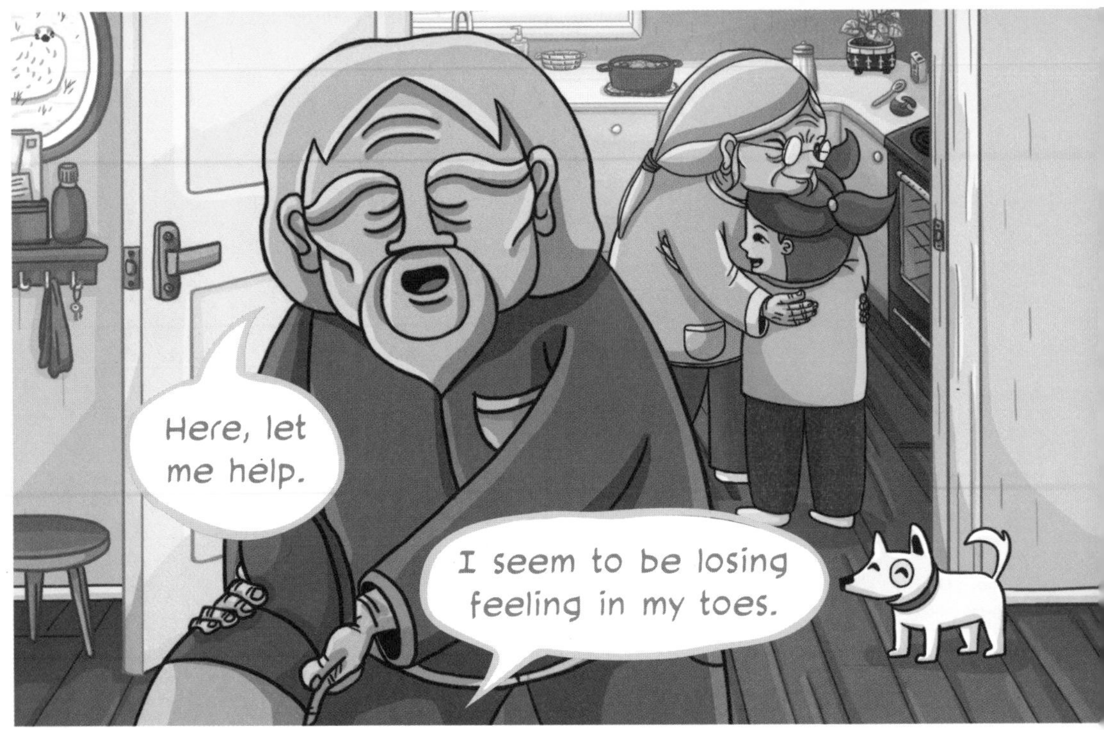
Here, let me help.
I seem to be losing feeling in my toes.

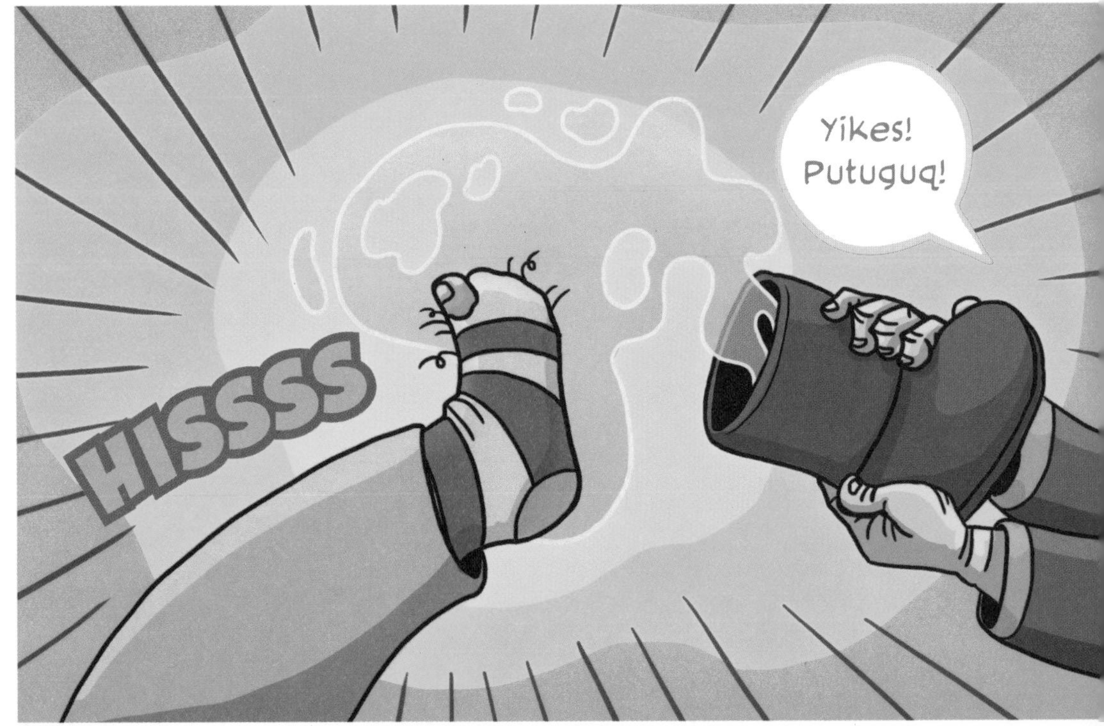
Yikes! Putuguq!
HISSSS

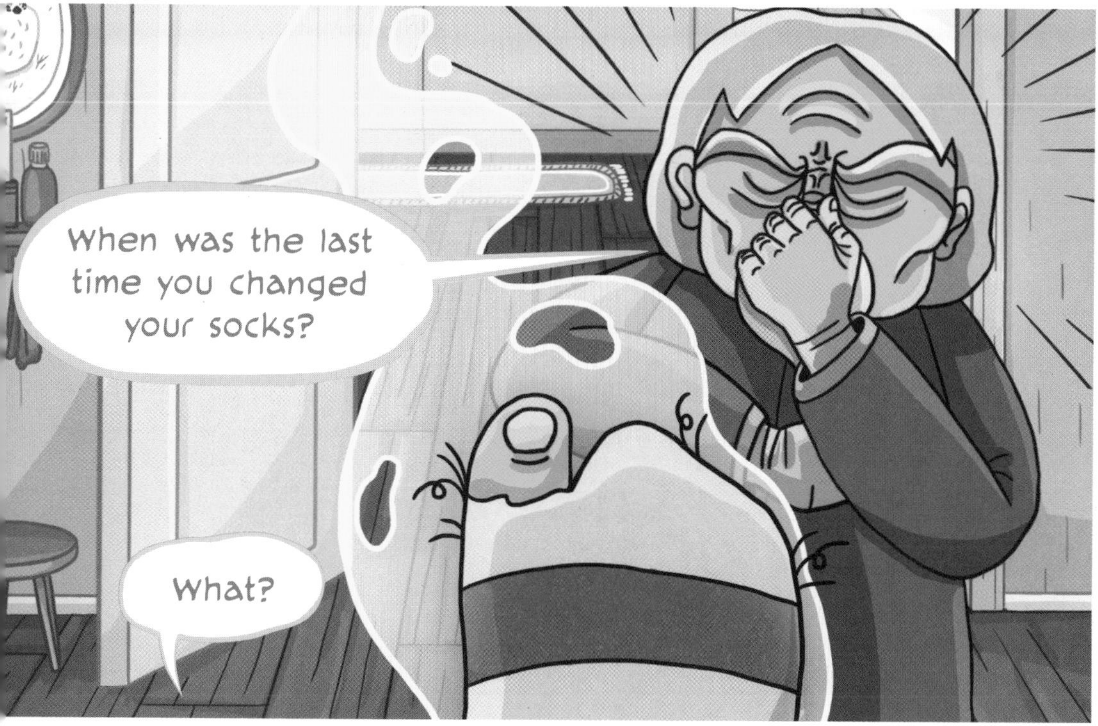
When was the last time you changed your socks?
What?

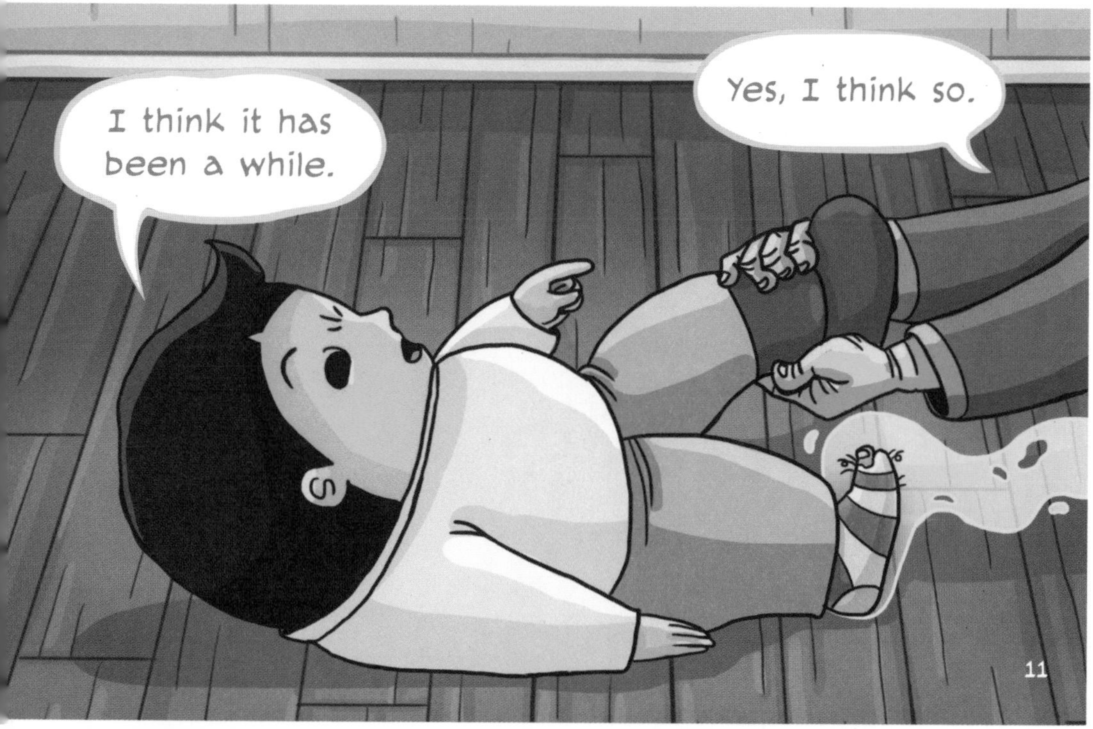
I think it has been a while.
Yes, I think so.

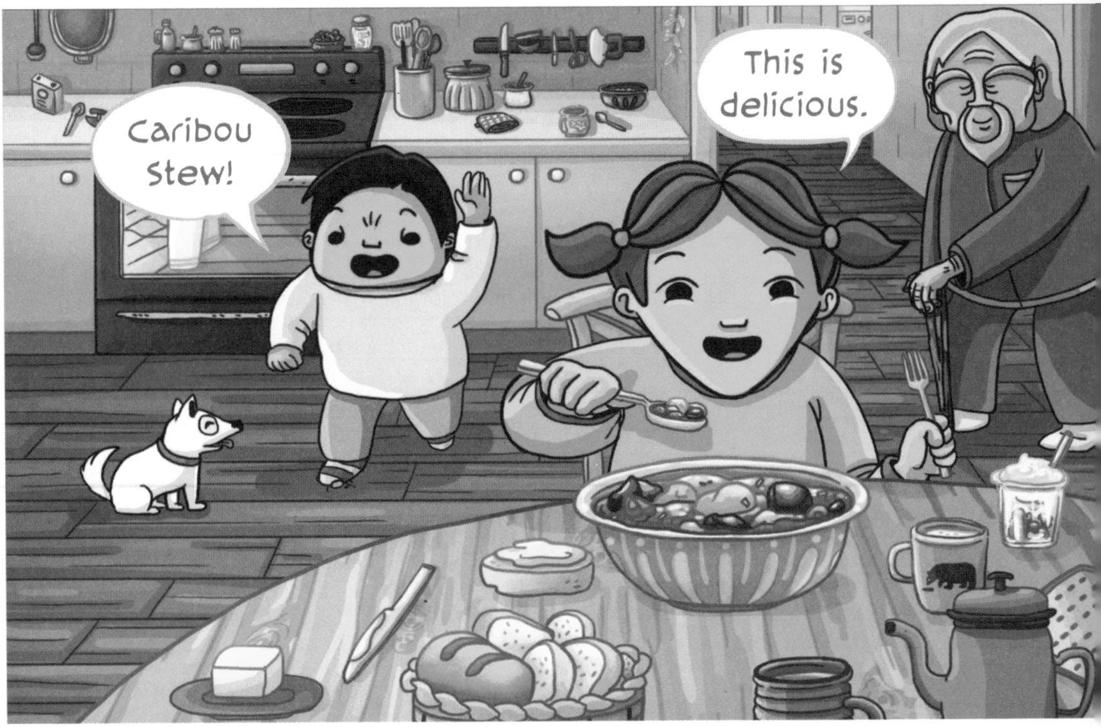
Caribou Stew!
This is delicious.

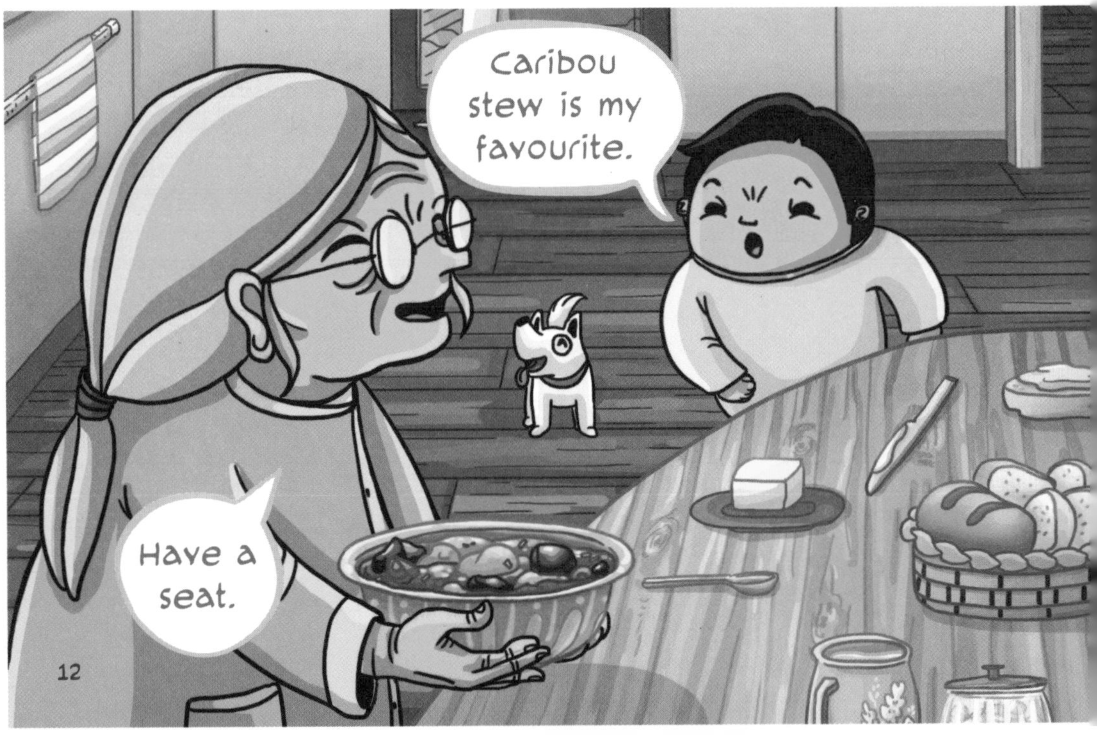
Caribou stew is my favourite.
Have a seat.

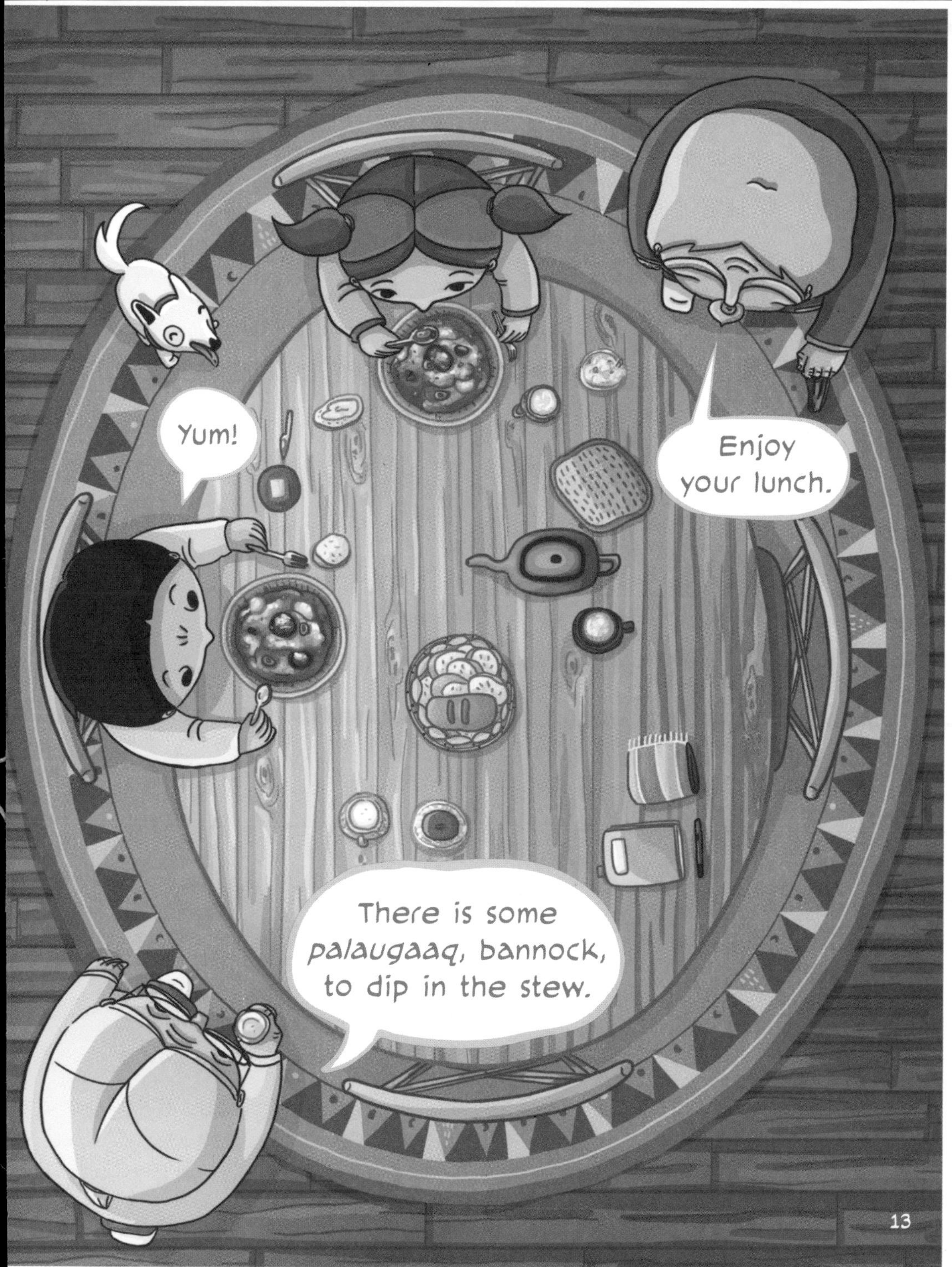
Yum!
Enjoy your lunch.
There is some *palaugaaq*, bannock, to dip in the stew.

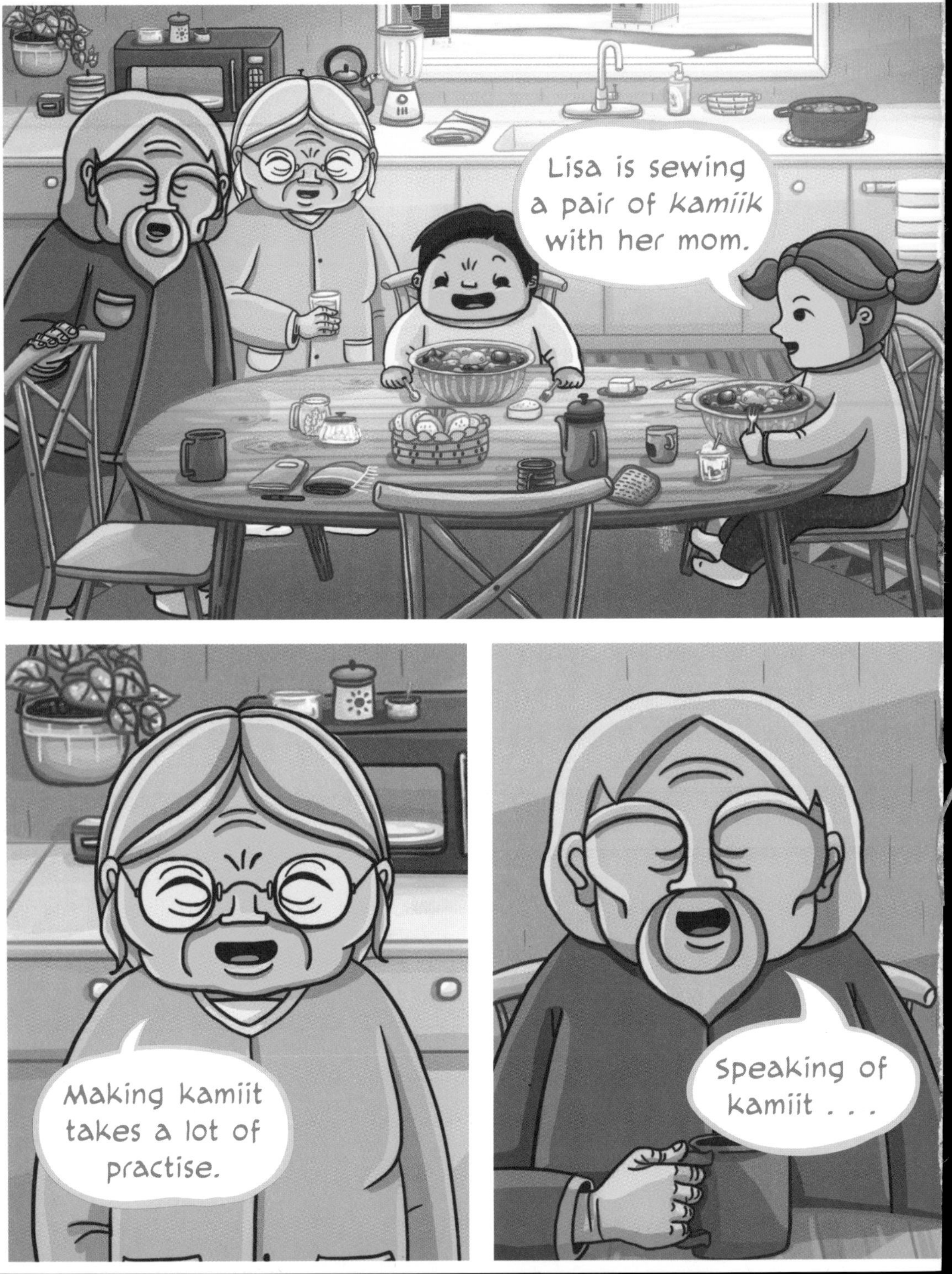
Lisa is sewing a pair of *kamiik* with her mom.
Making kamiit takes a lot of practise.
Speaking of kamiit . . .

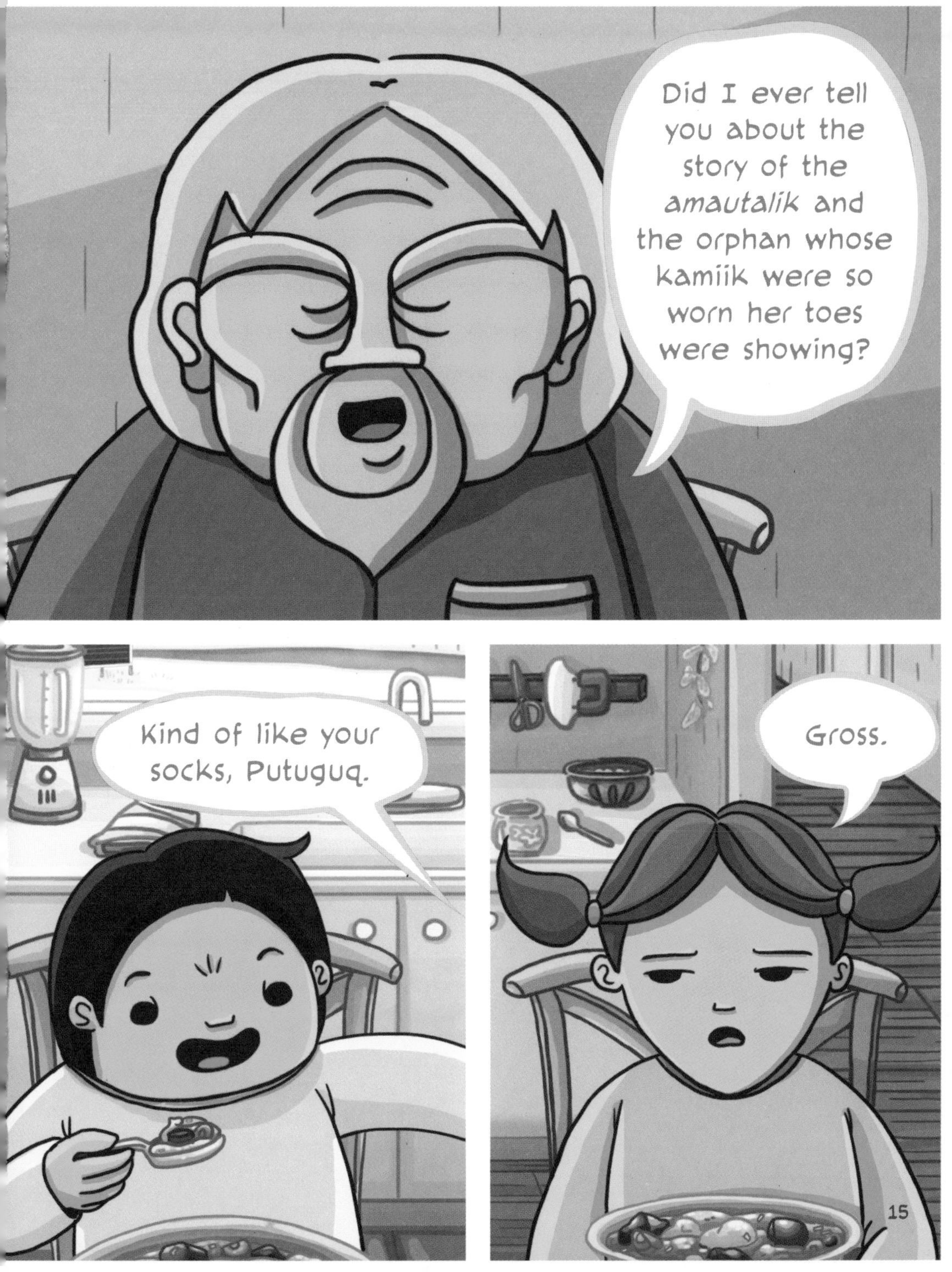
Did I ever tell you about the story of the *amautalik* and the orphan whose kamiik were so worn her toes were showing?
Kind of like your socks, Putuguq.
Gross.

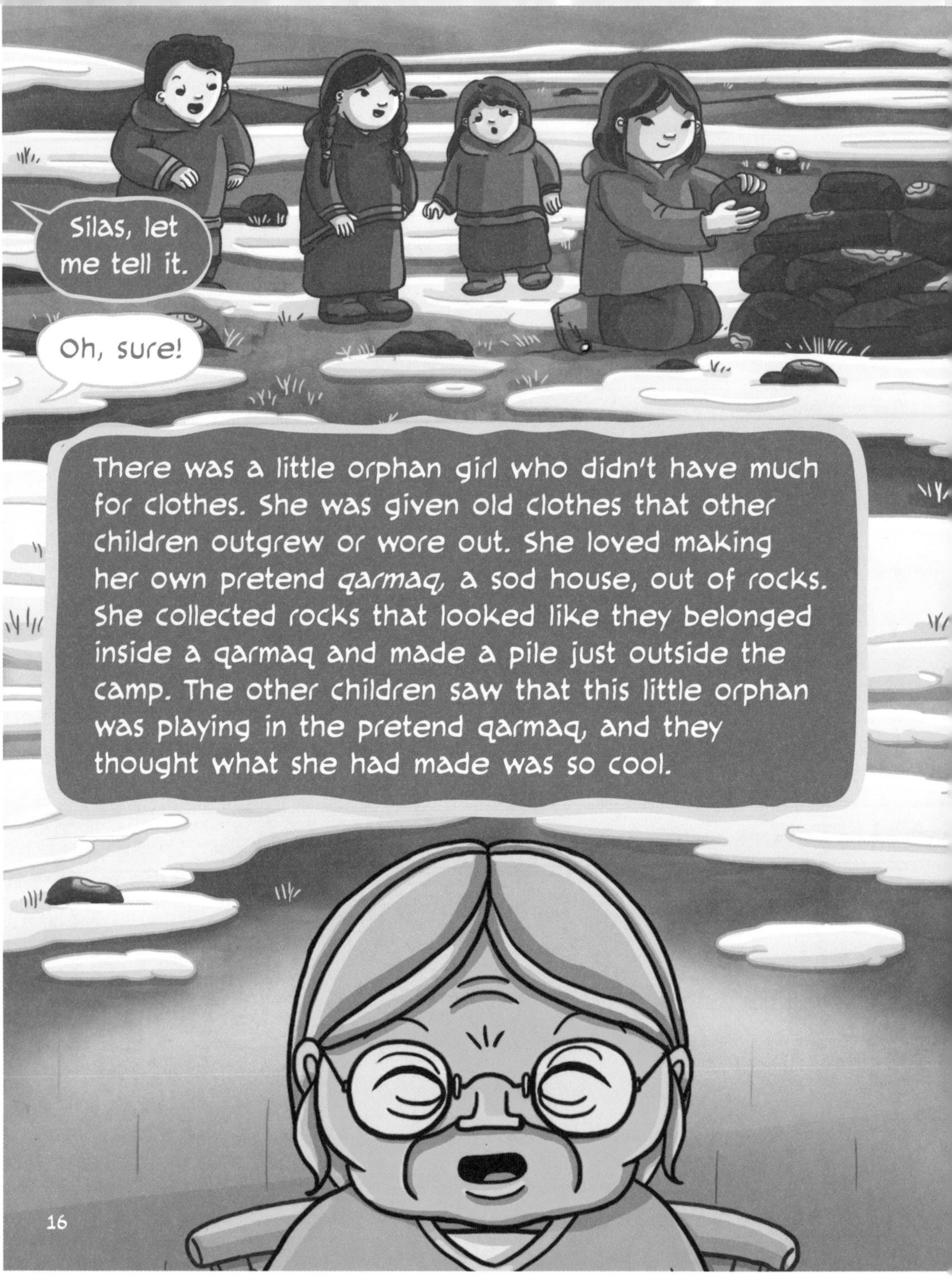
Silas, let me tell it.
Oh, sure!
There was a little orphan girl who didn't have much for clothes. She was given old clothes that other children outgrew or wore out. She loved making her own pretend *qarmaq*, a sod house, out of rocks. She collected rocks that looked like they belonged inside a qarmaq and made a pile just outside the camp. The other children saw that this little orphan was playing in the pretend qarmaq, and they thought what she had made was so cool.

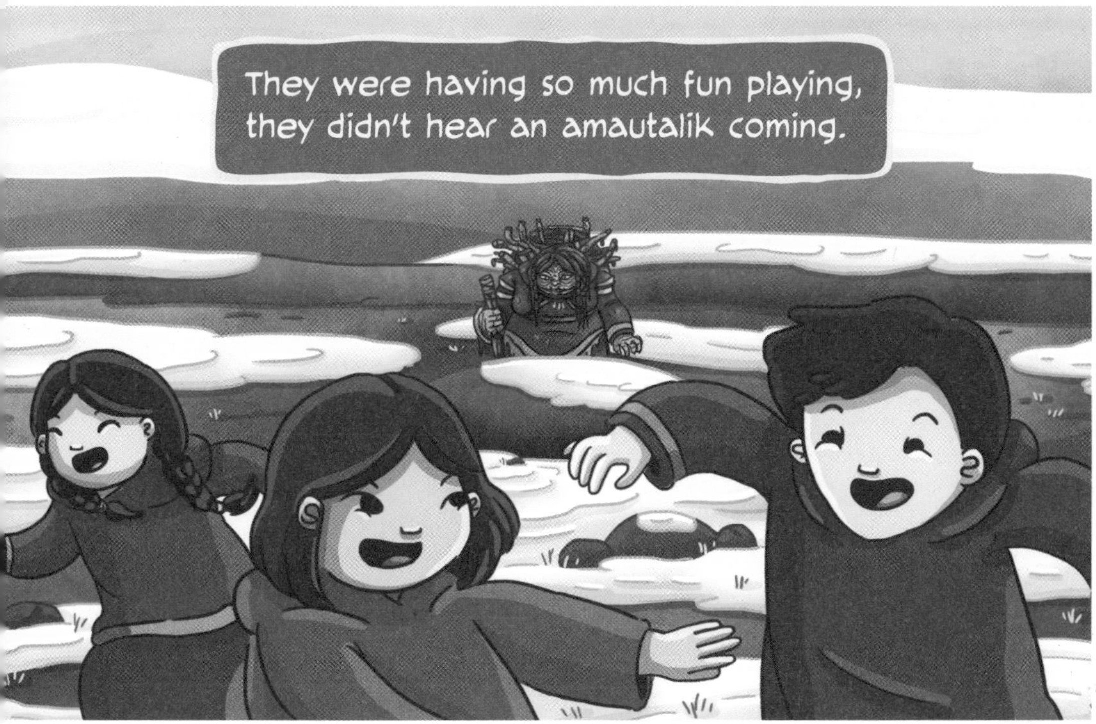
They were having so much fun playing, they didn't hear an amautalik coming.

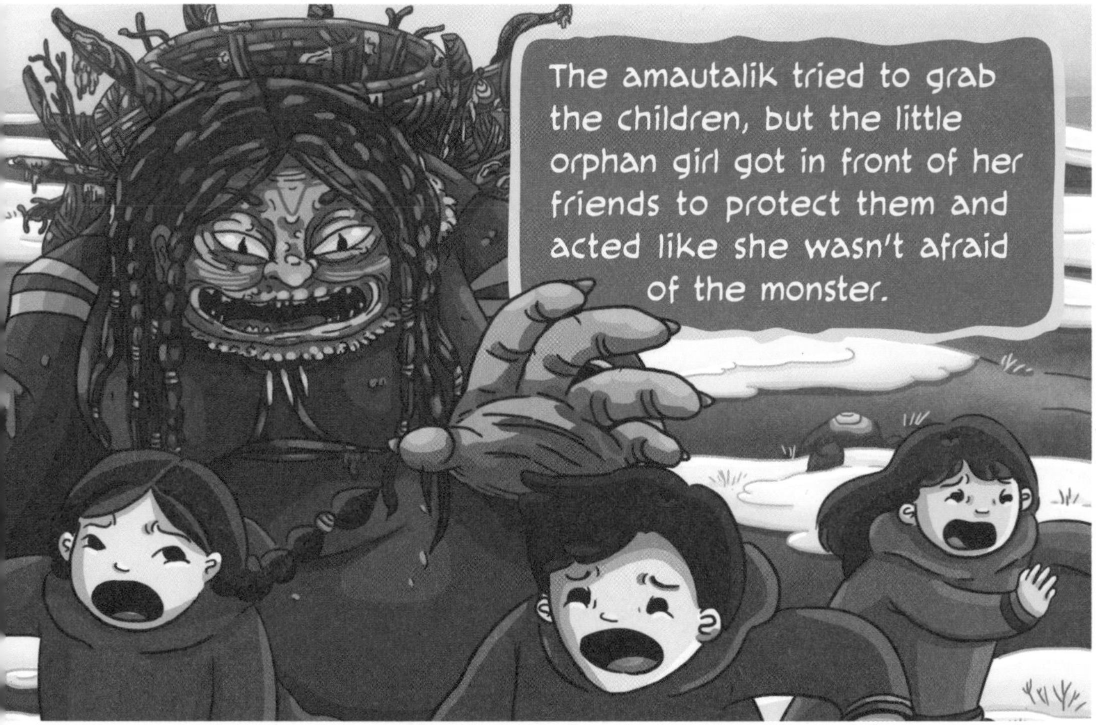
The amautalik tried to grab the children, but the little orphan girl got in front of her friends to protect them and acted like she wasn't afraid of the monster.

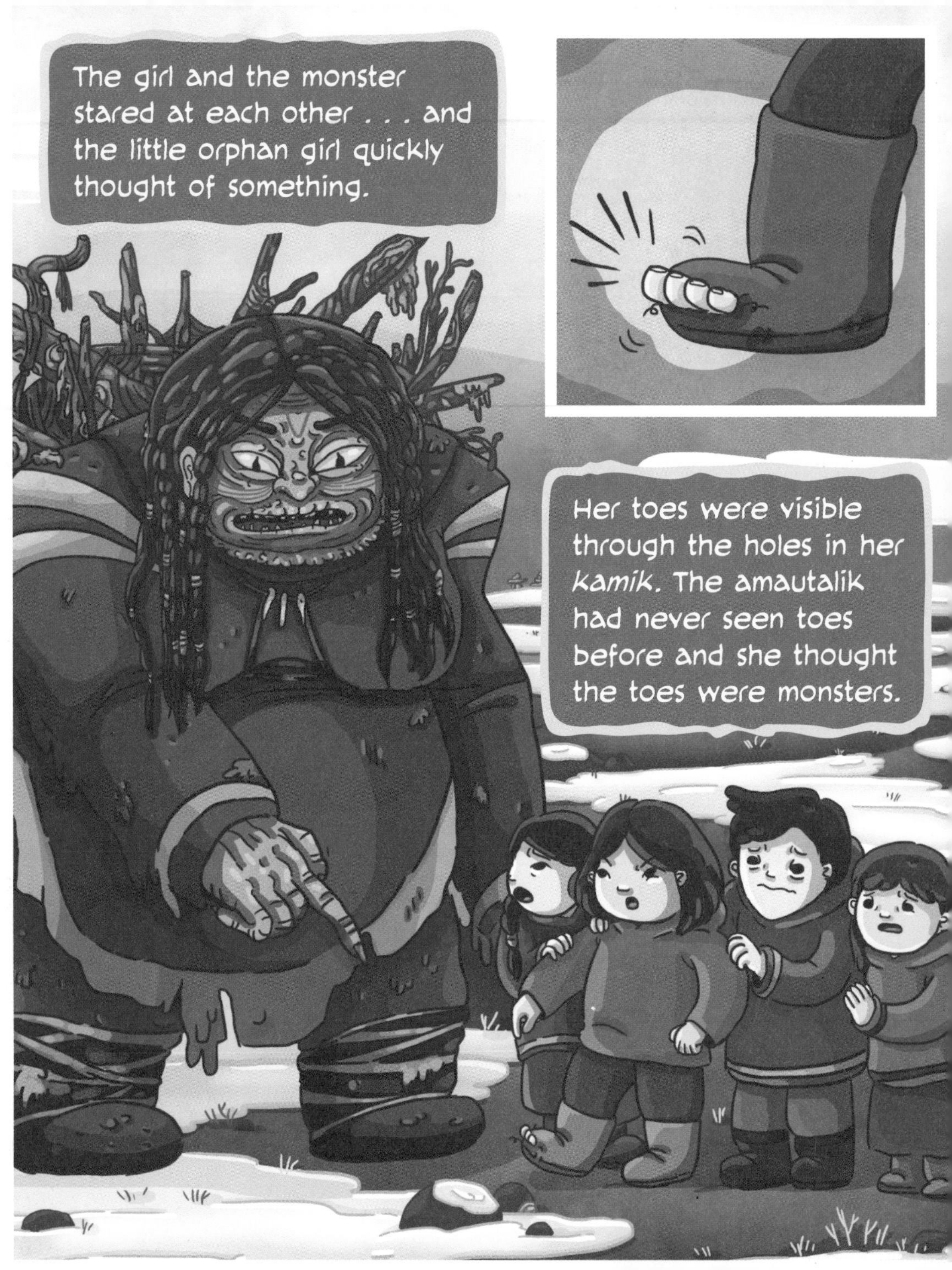
The girl and the monster stared at each other . . . and the little orphan girl quickly thought of something.
Her toes were visible through the holes in her *kamik*. The amautalik had never seen toes before and she thought the toes were monsters.

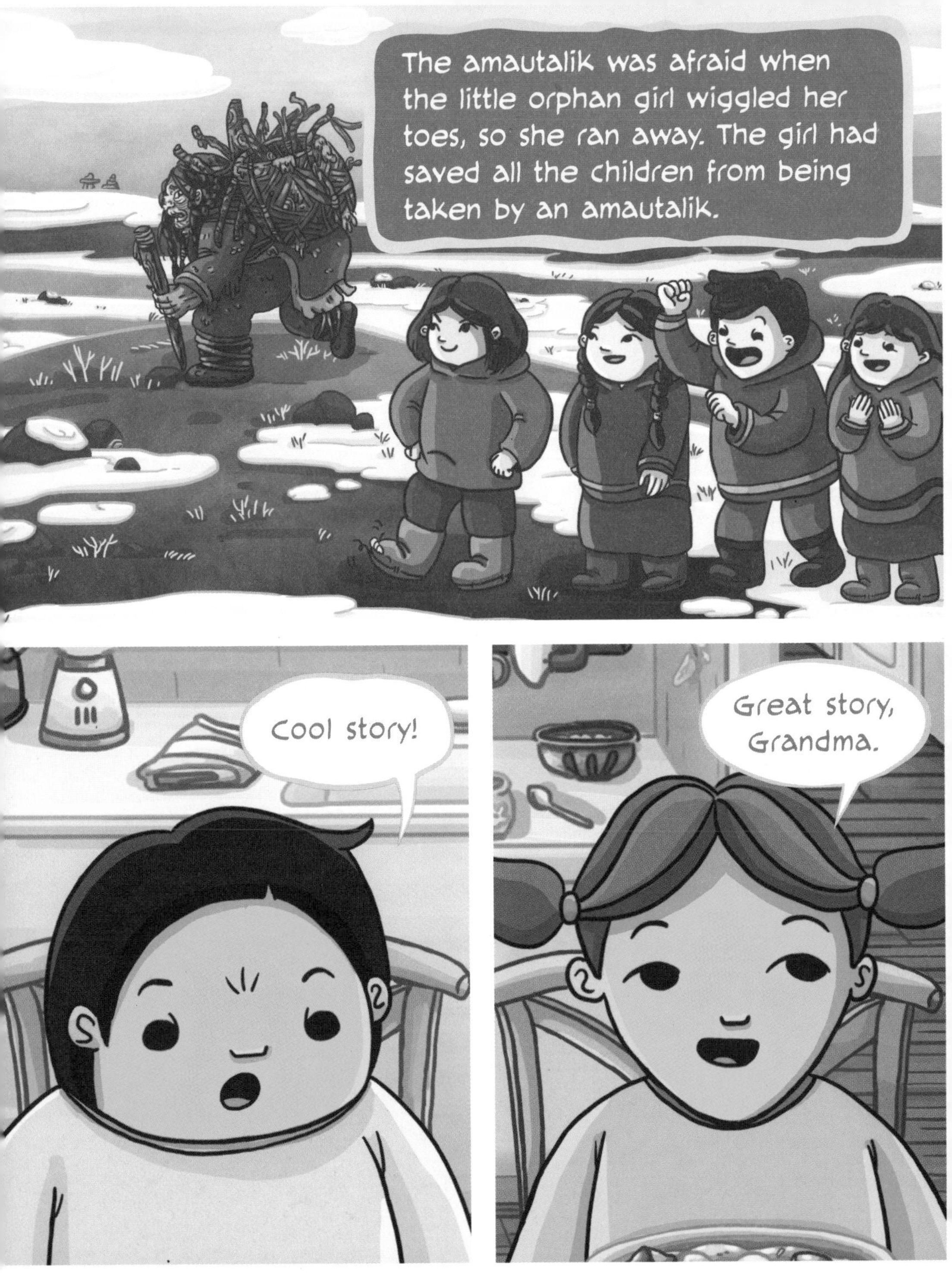
The amautalik was afraid when the little orphan girl wiggled her toes, so she ran away. The girl had saved all the children from being taken by an amautalik.
Cool story!
Great story, Grandma.

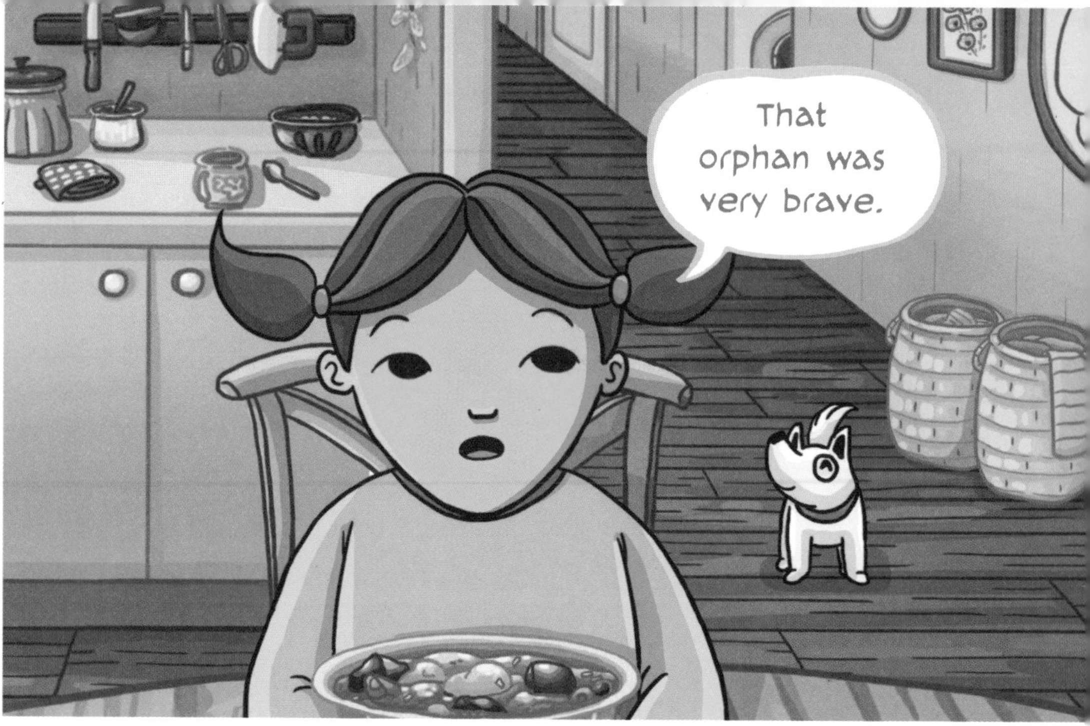
That orphan was very brave.

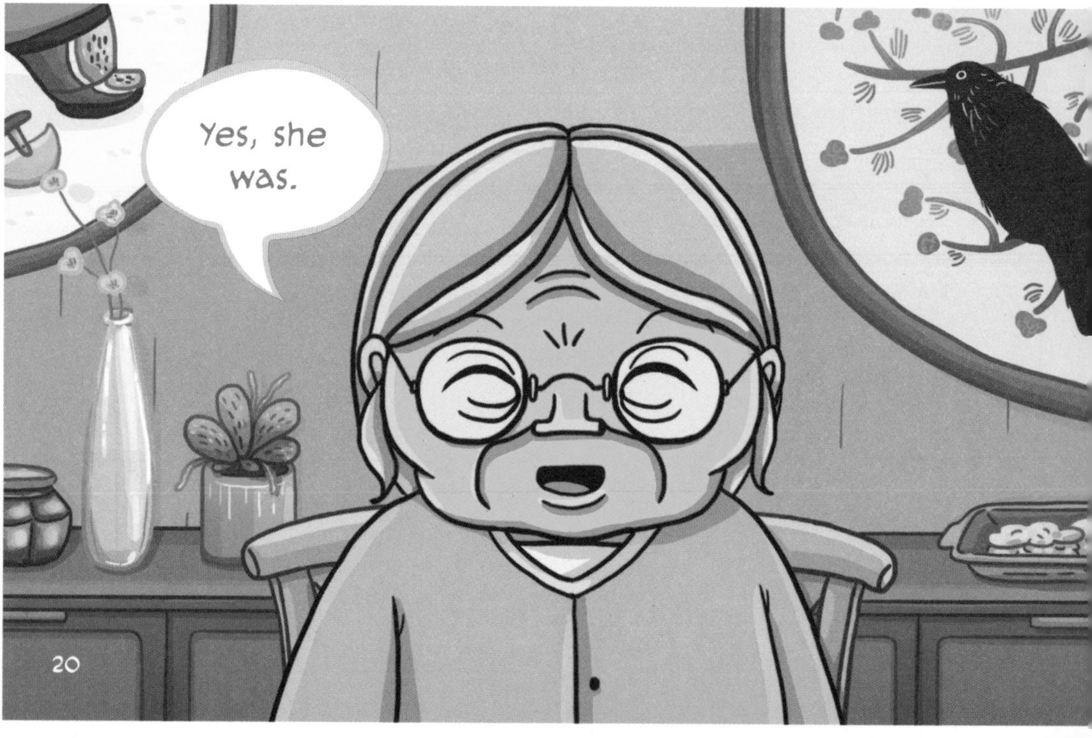
Yes, she was.

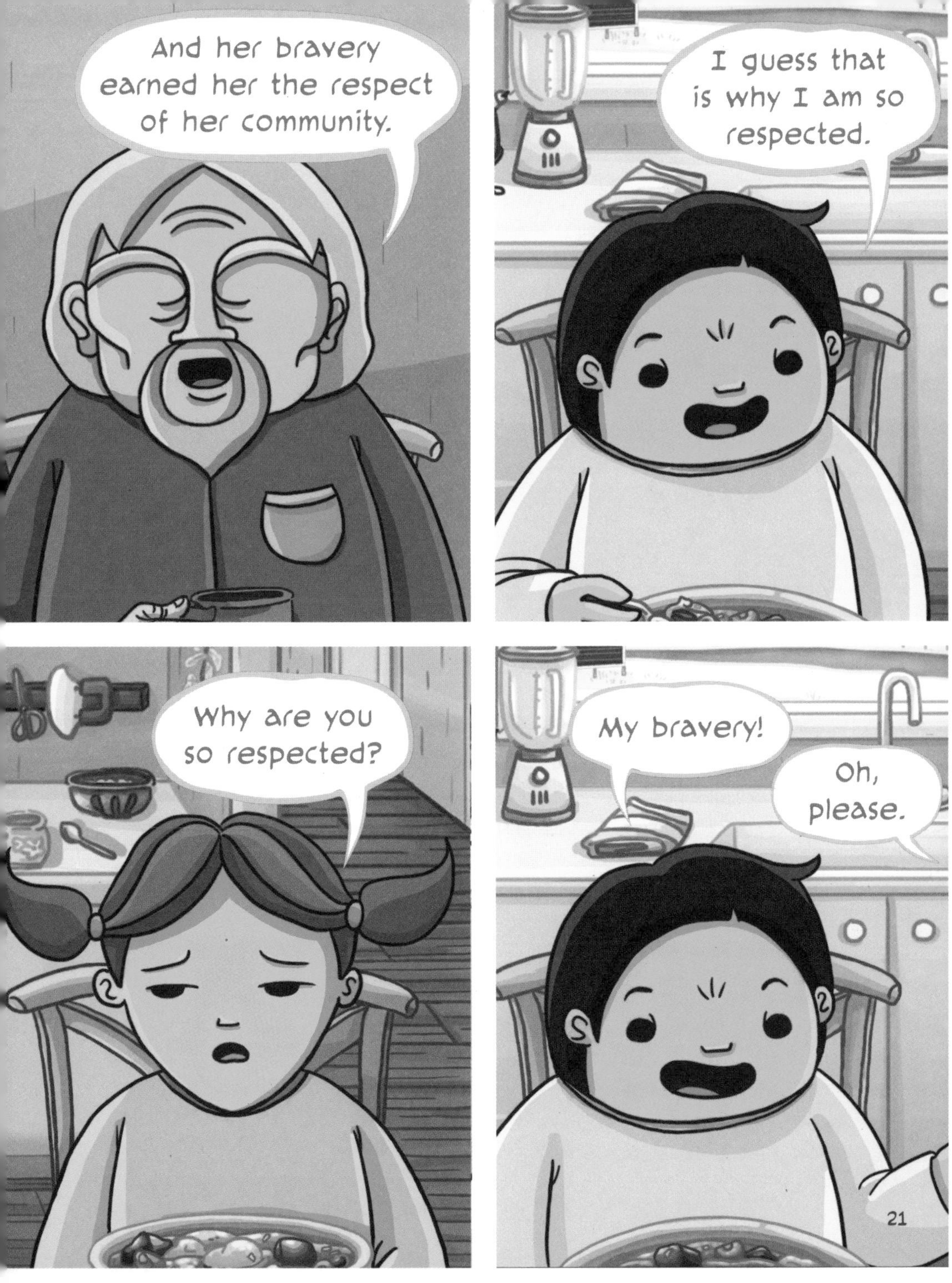
And her bravery earned her the respect of her community.
I guess that is why I am so respected.
Why are you so respected?
My bravery!
Oh, please.

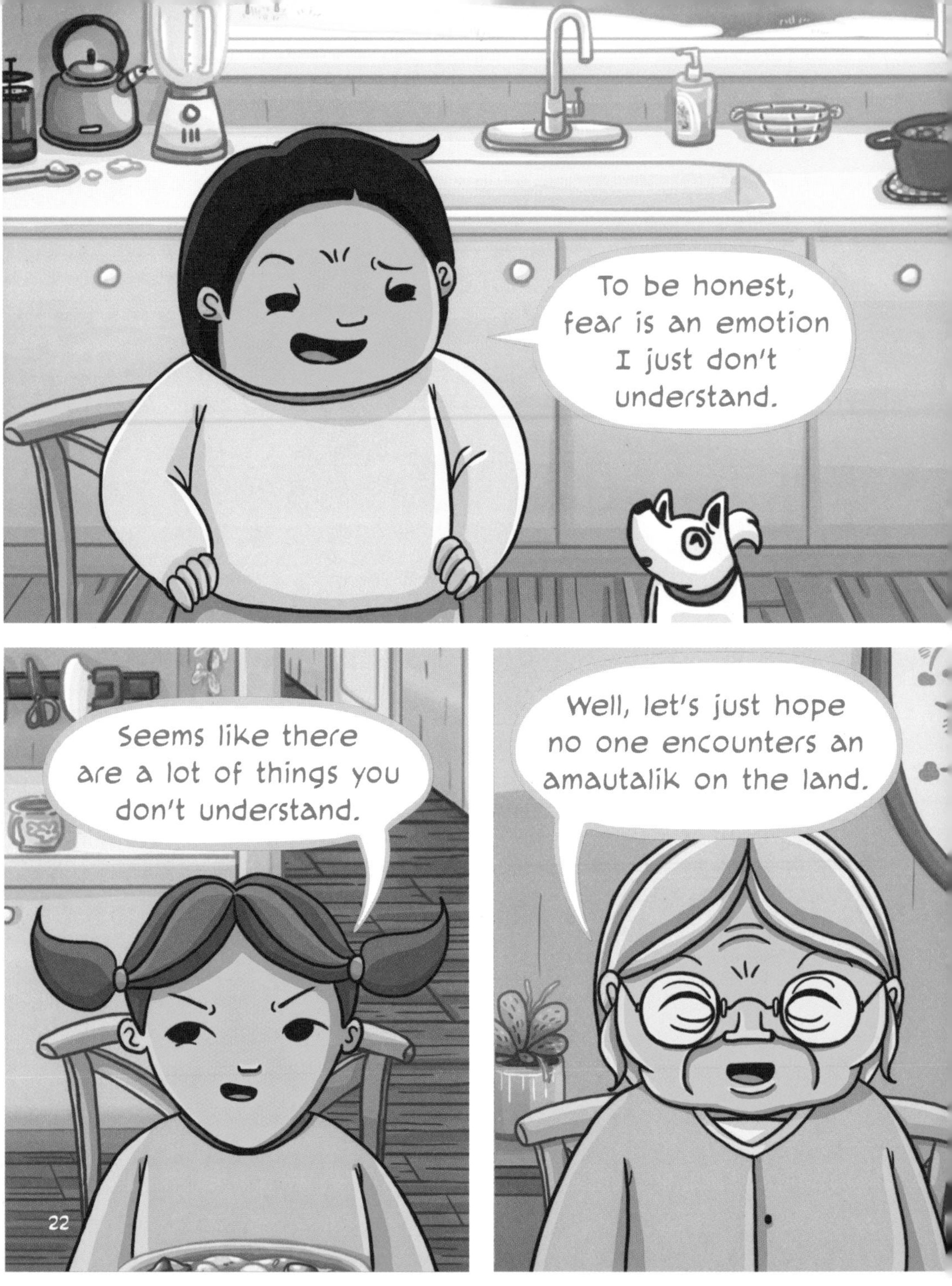
To be honest, fear is an emotion I just don't understand.
Seems like there are a lot of things you don't understand.
Well, let's just hope no one encounters an amautalik on the land.

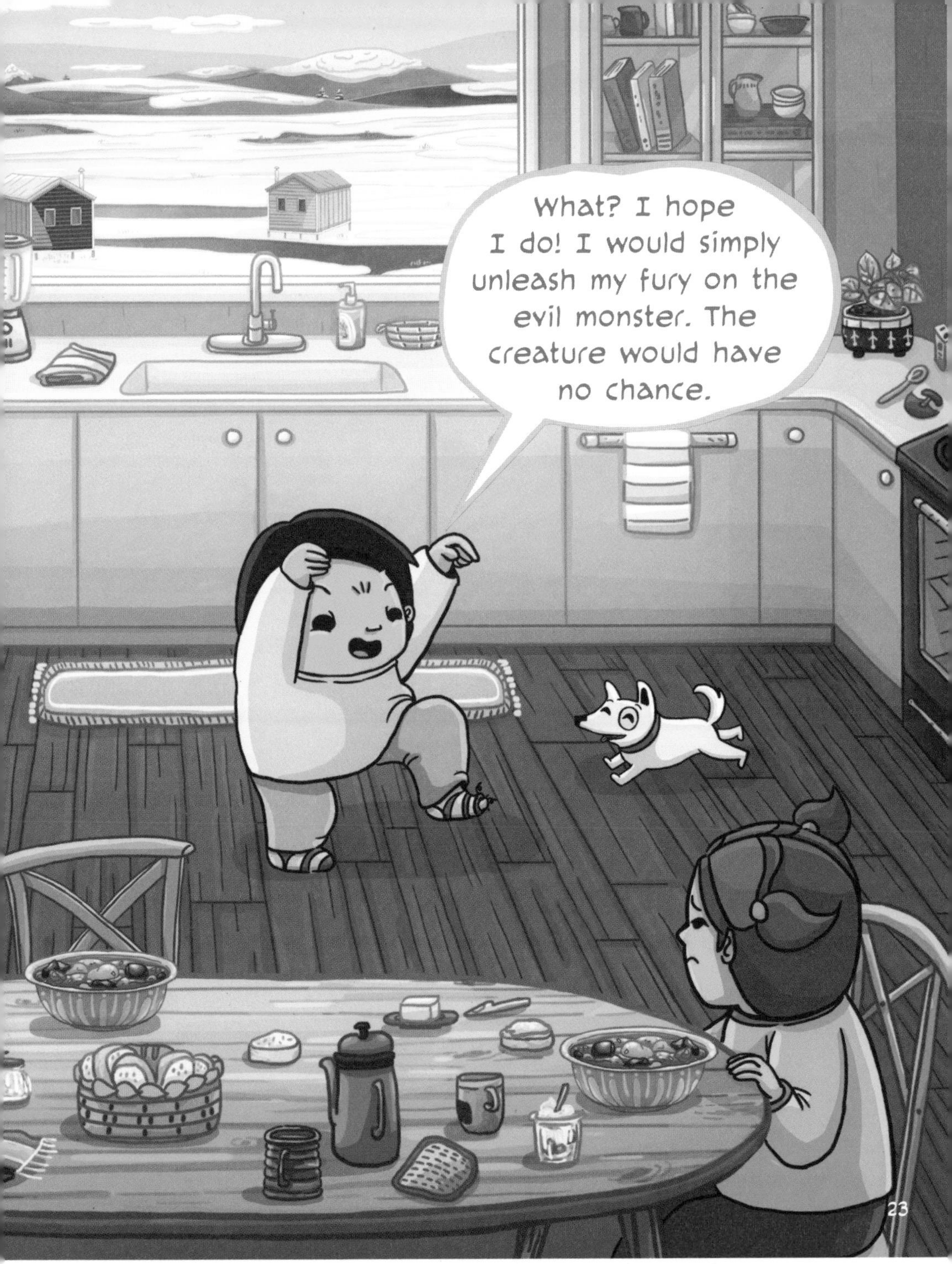
What? I hope I do! I would simply unleash my fury on the evil monster. The creature would have no chance.

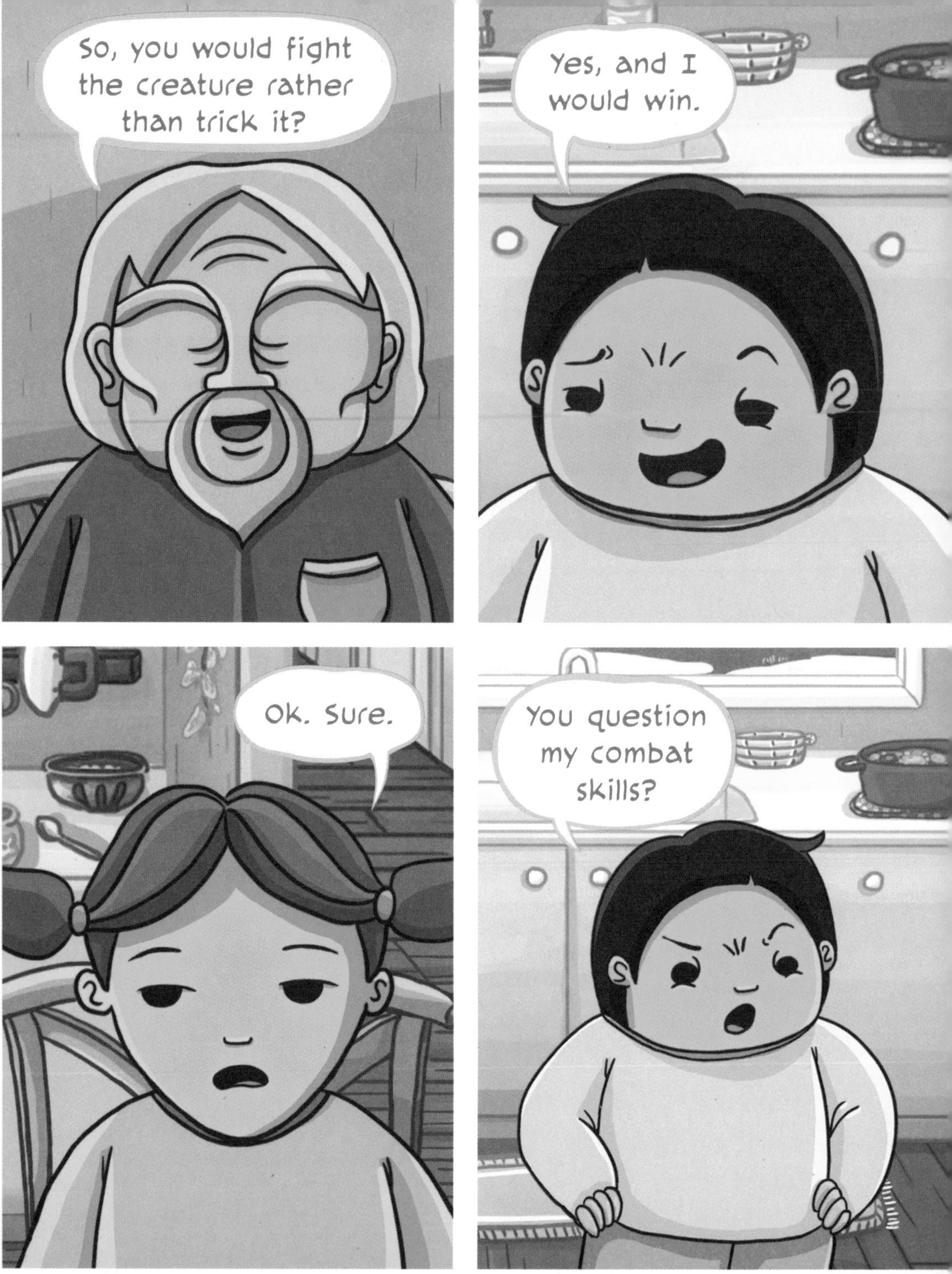
So, you would fight the creature rather than trick it?
Yes, and I would win.
Ok. Sure.
You question my combat skills?

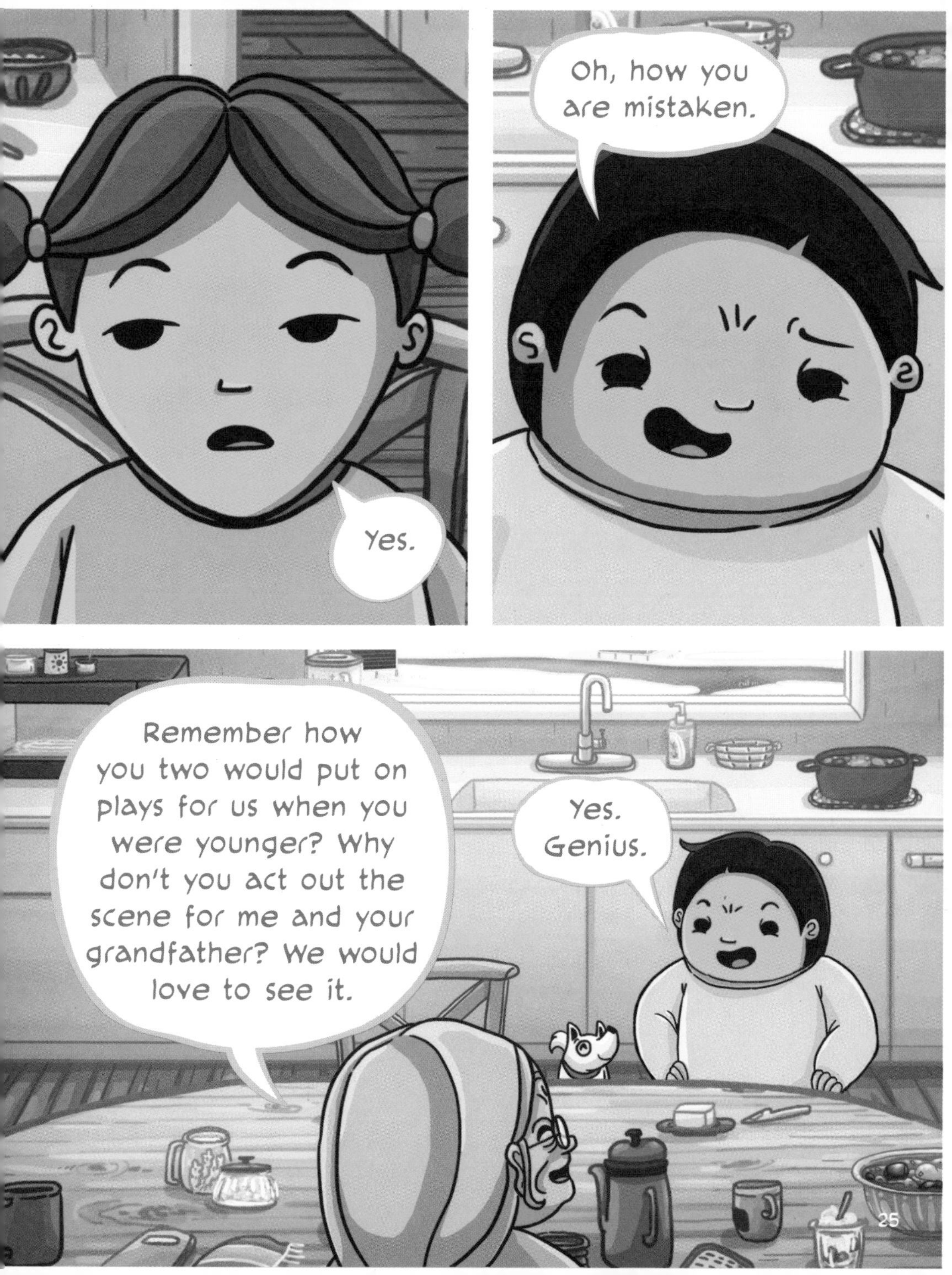
Yes.
Oh, how you are mistaken.
Remember how you two would put on plays for us when you were younger? Why don't you act out the scene for me and your grandfather? We would love to see it.
Yes. Genius.

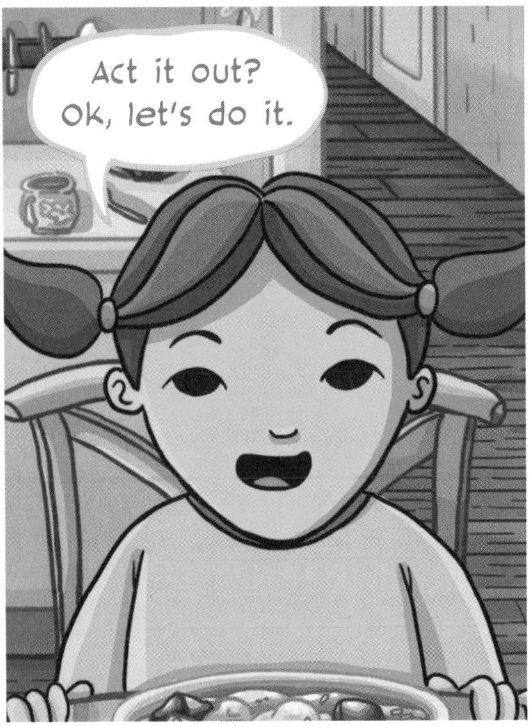
Act it out? Ok, let's do it.

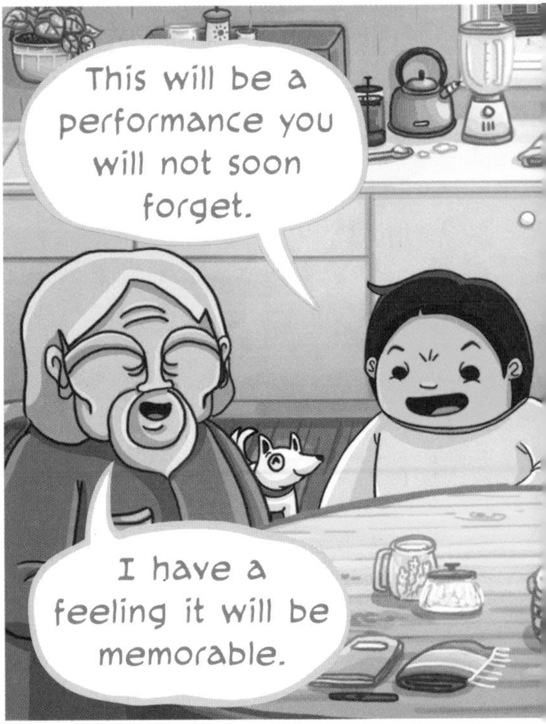
This will be a performance you will not soon forget.
I have a feeling it will be memorable.

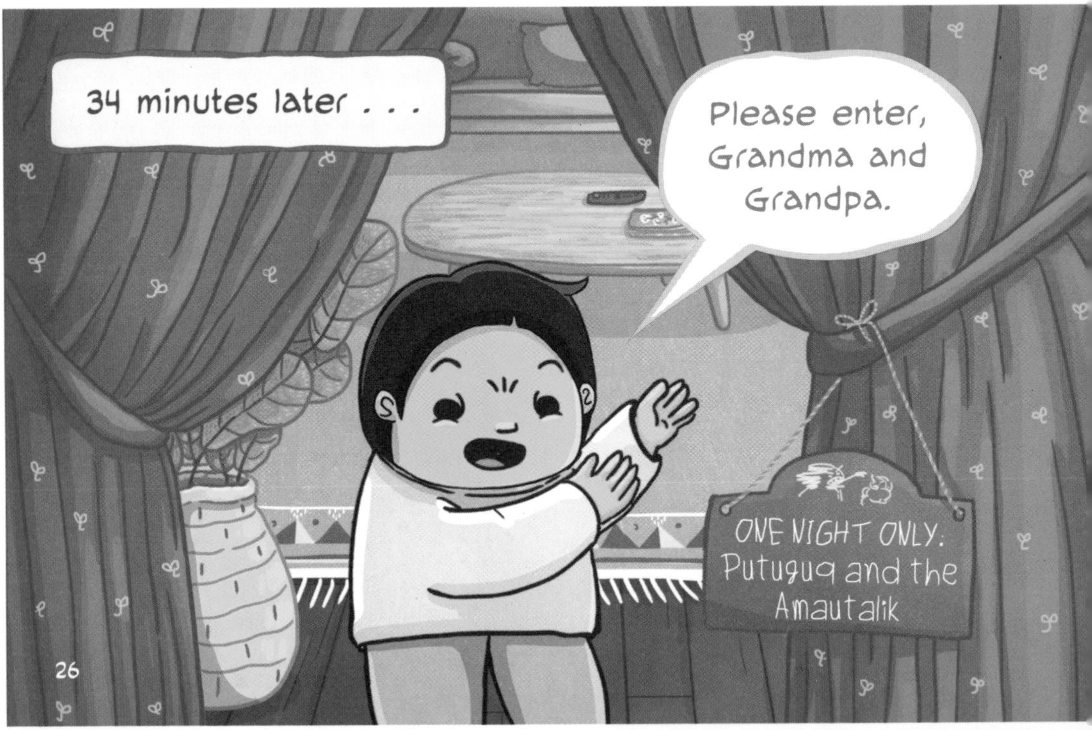
34 minutes later . . .
Please enter, Grandma and Grandpa.
ONE NIGHT ONLY: Putuguq and the Amautalik

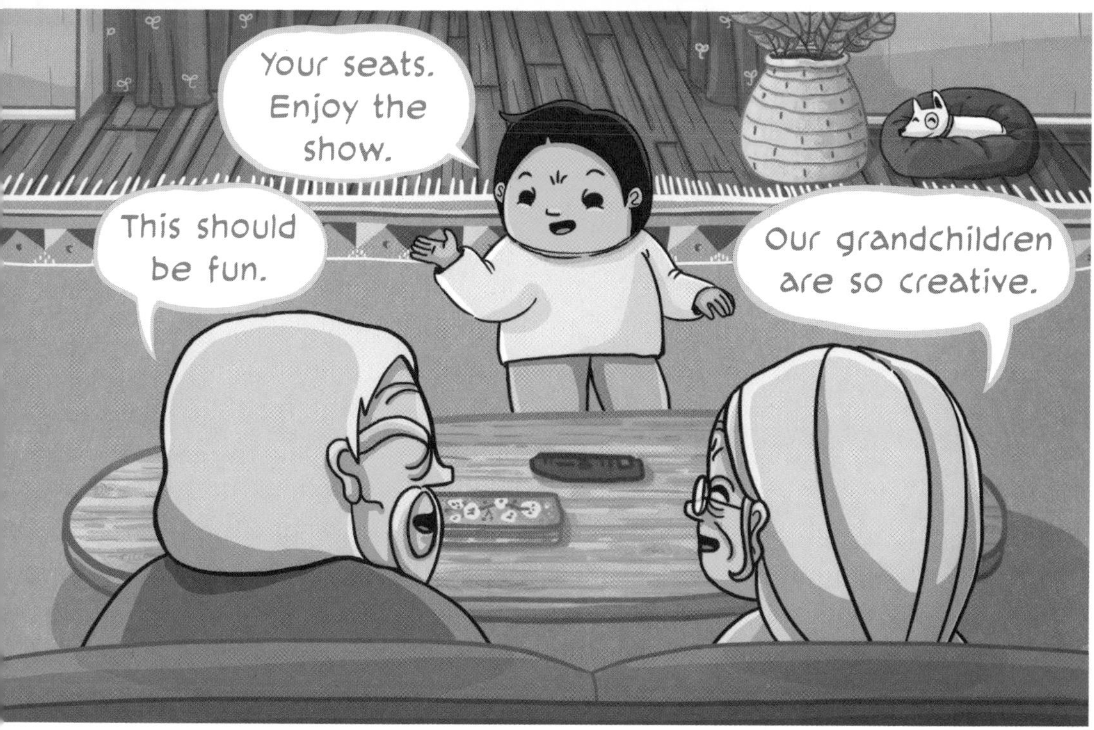
Your seats. Enjoy the show.
This should be fun.
Our grandchildren are so creative.

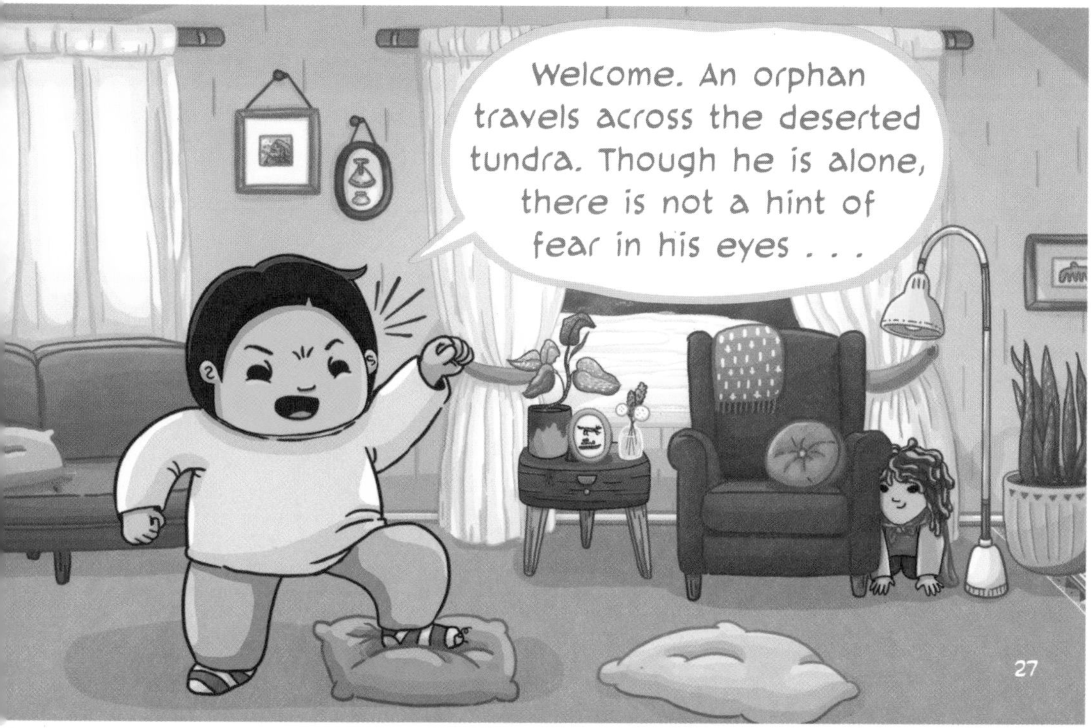
Welcome. An orphan travels across the deserted tundra. Though he is alone, there is not a hint of fear in his eyes . . .

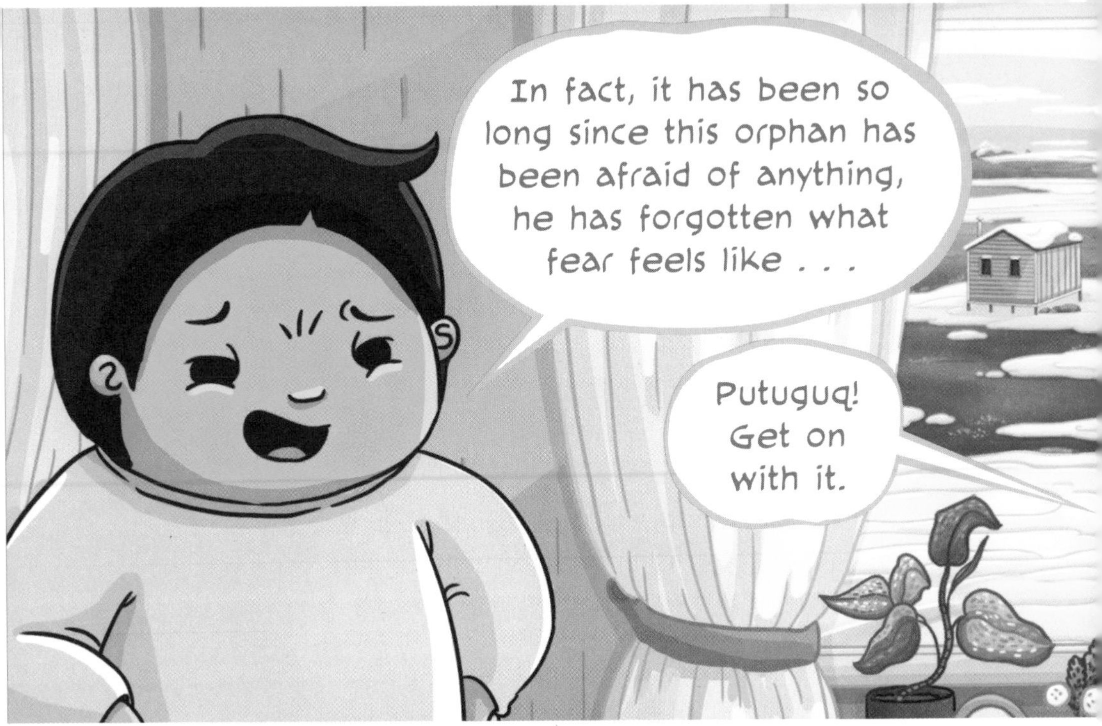
In fact, it has been so long since this orphan has been afraid of anything, he has forgotten what fear feels like . . .
Putuguq! Get on with it.

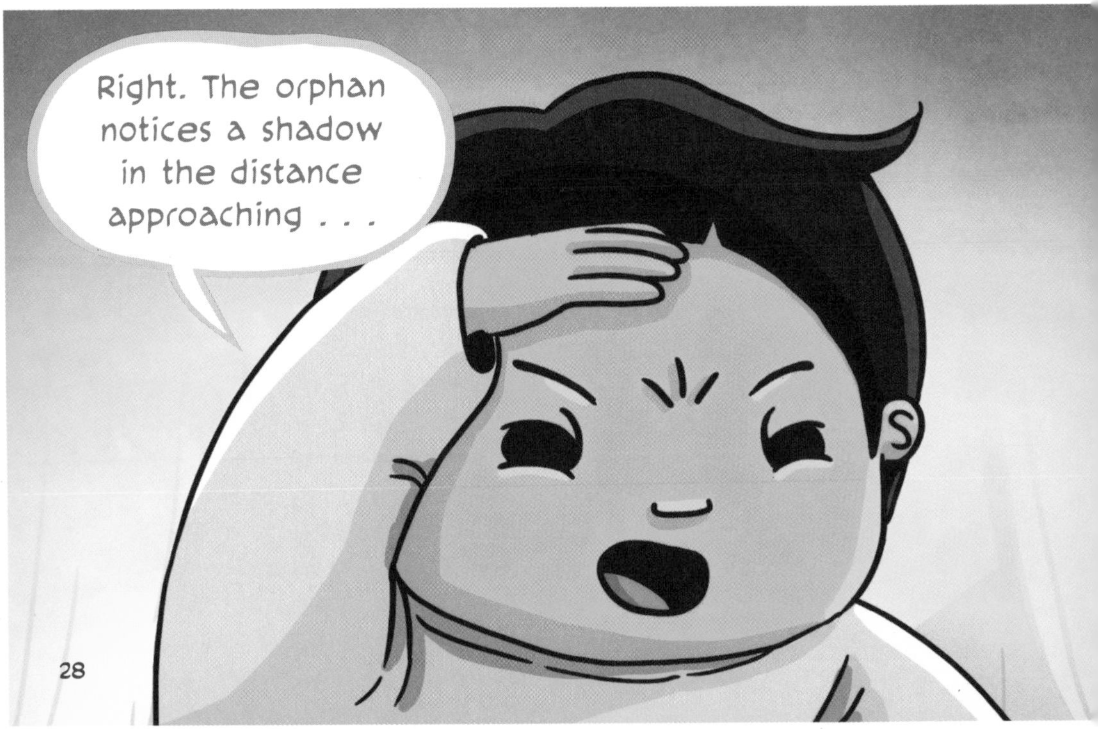
Right. The orphan notices a shadow in the distance approaching . . .

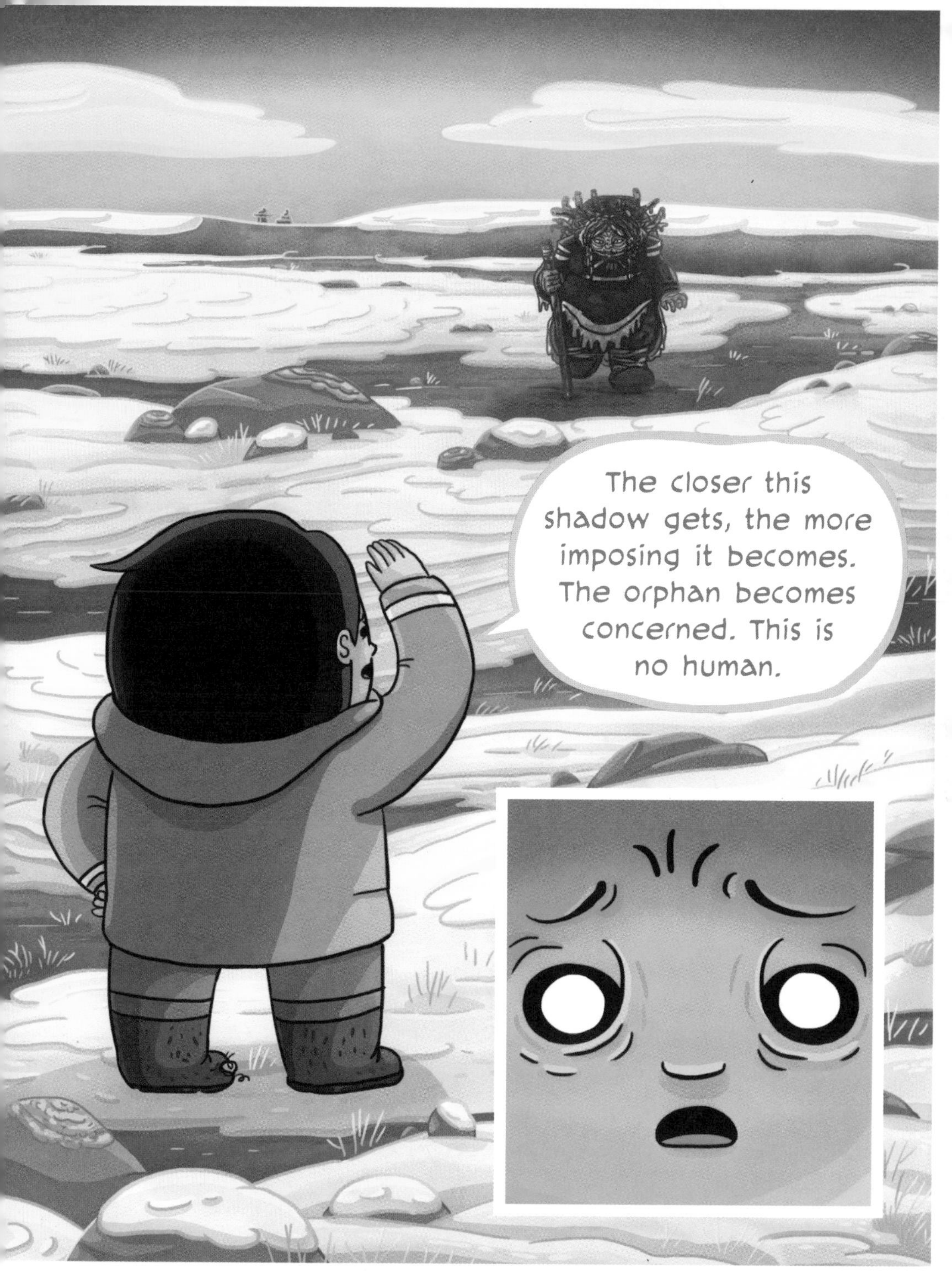

The closer this shadow gets, the more imposing it becomes. The orphan becomes concerned. This is no human.

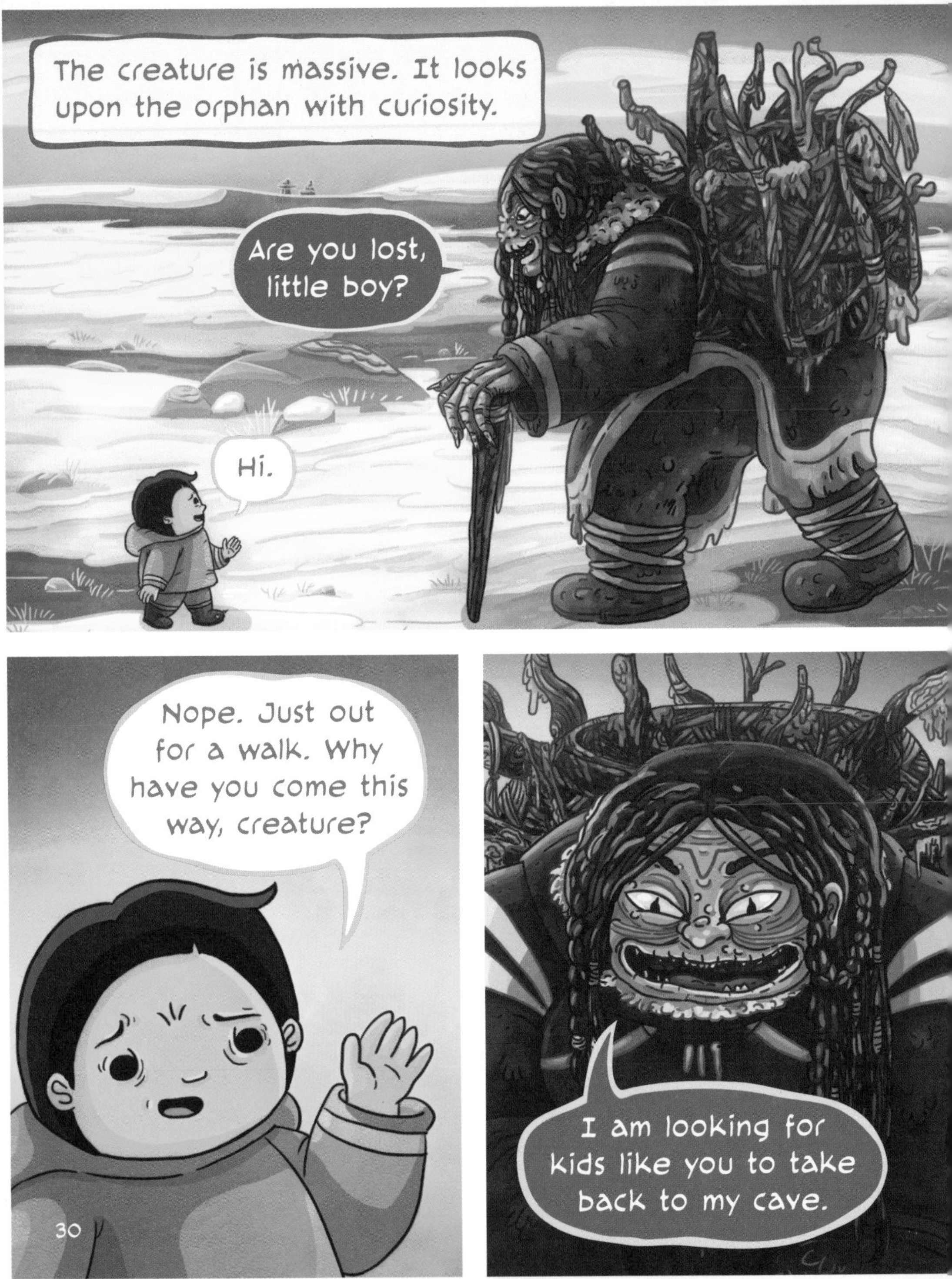
The creature is massive. It looks upon the orphan with curiosity.
Are you lost, little boy?
Hi.
Nope. Just out for a walk. Why have you come this way, creature?
I am looking for kids like you to take back to my cave.

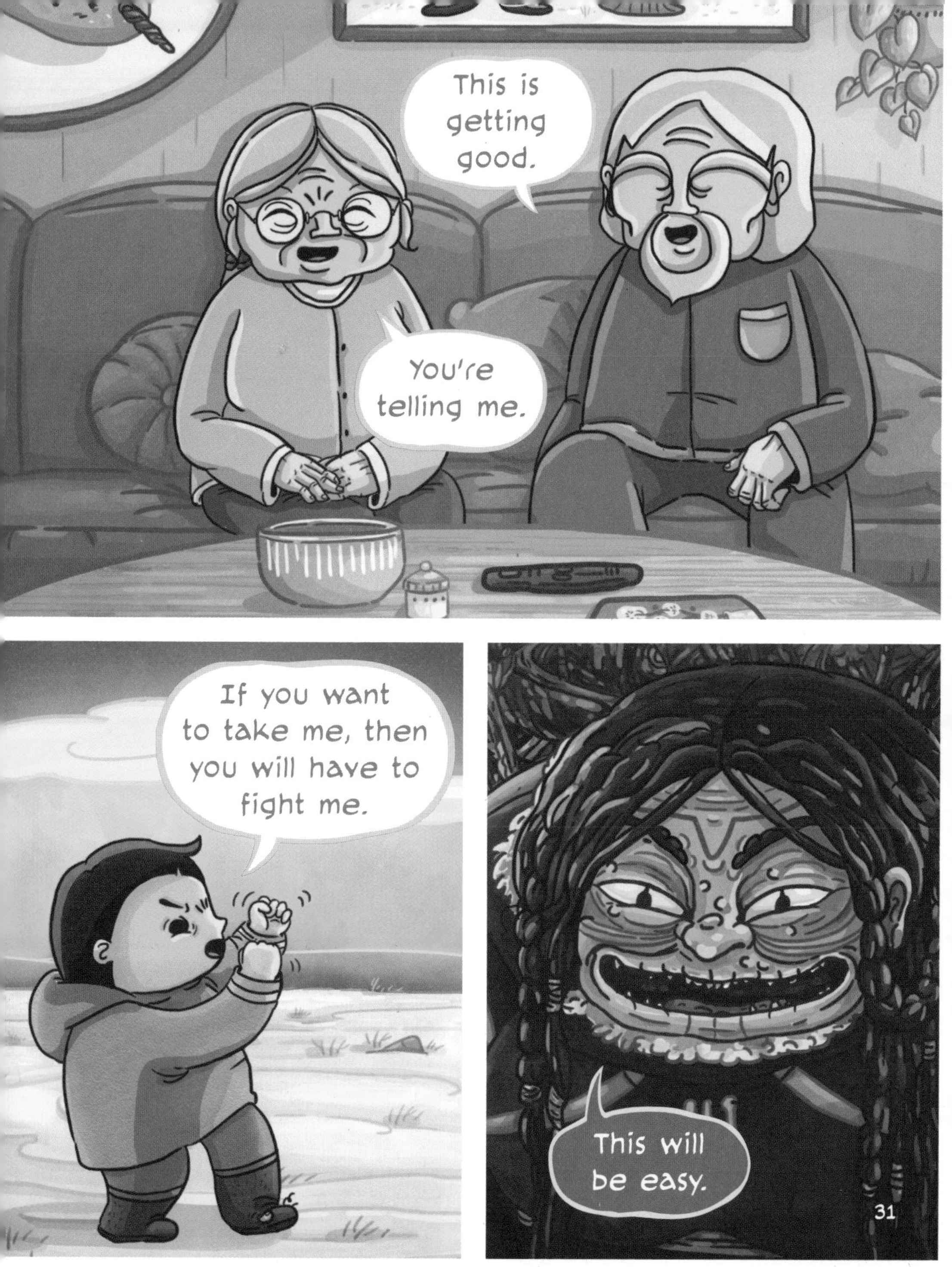
This is getting good.
You're telling me.
If you want to take me, then you will have to fight me.
This will be easy.

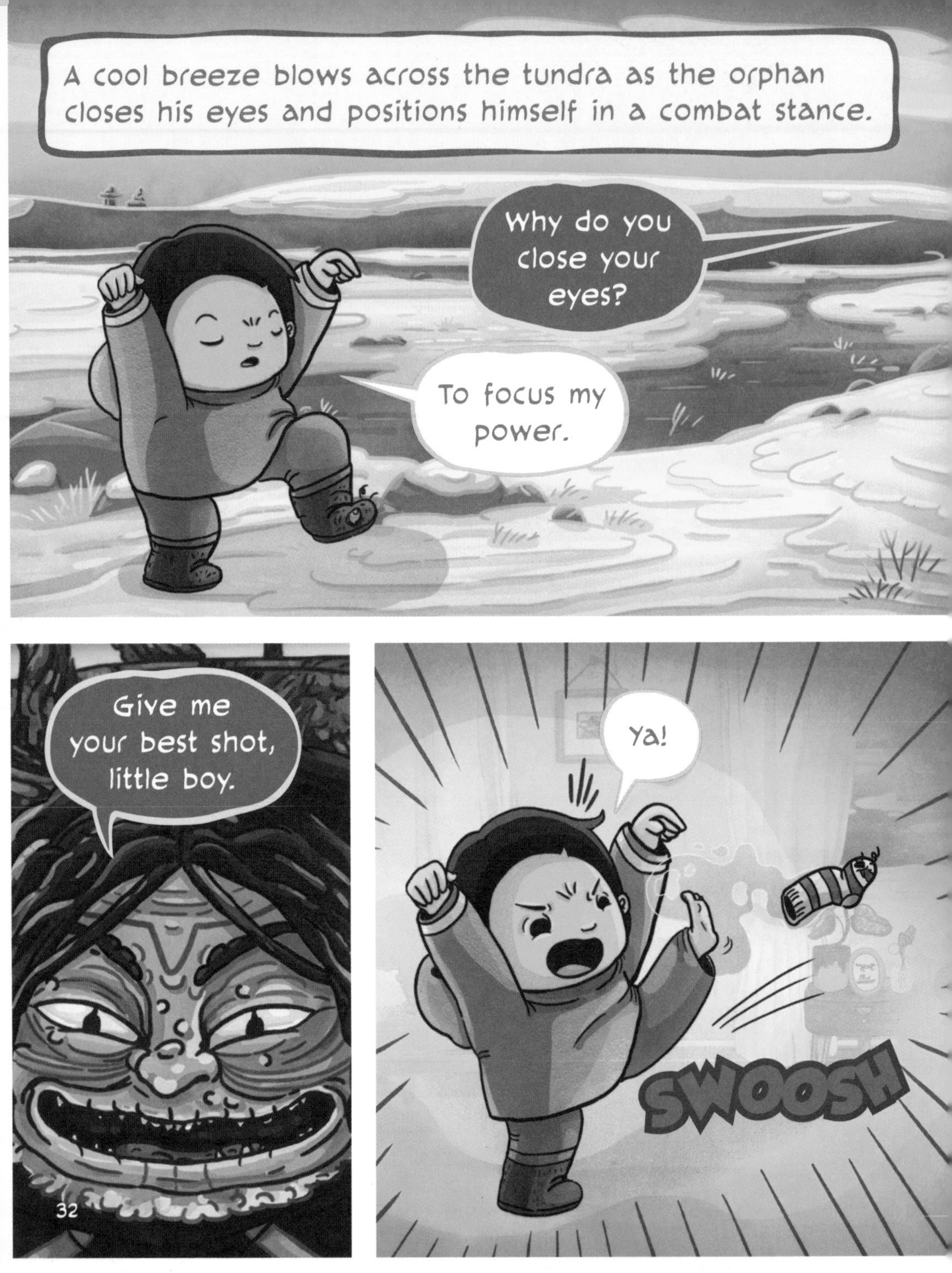
A cool breeze blows across the tundra as the orphan closes his eyes and positions himself in a combat stance.
Why do you close your eyes?
To focus my power.
Give me your best shot, little boy.
Ya!
SWOOSH

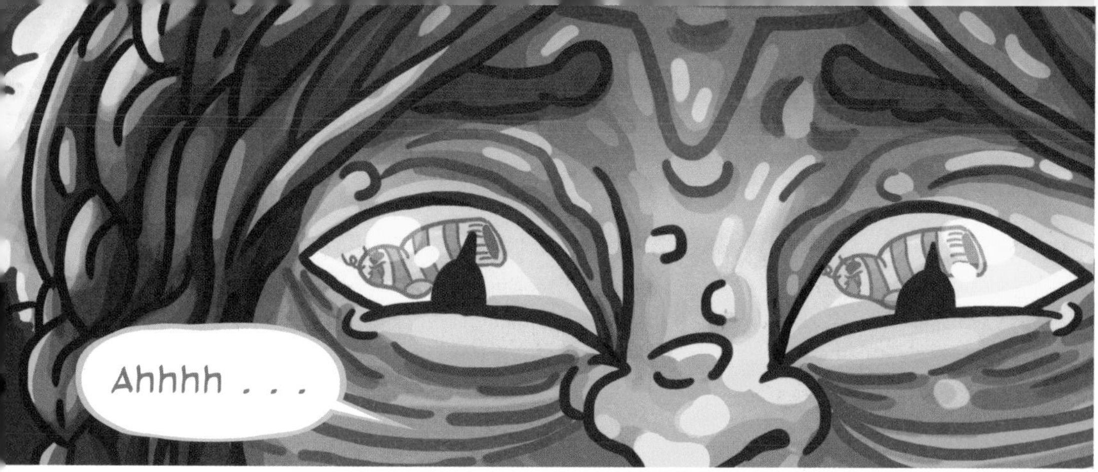
Ahhhh . . .

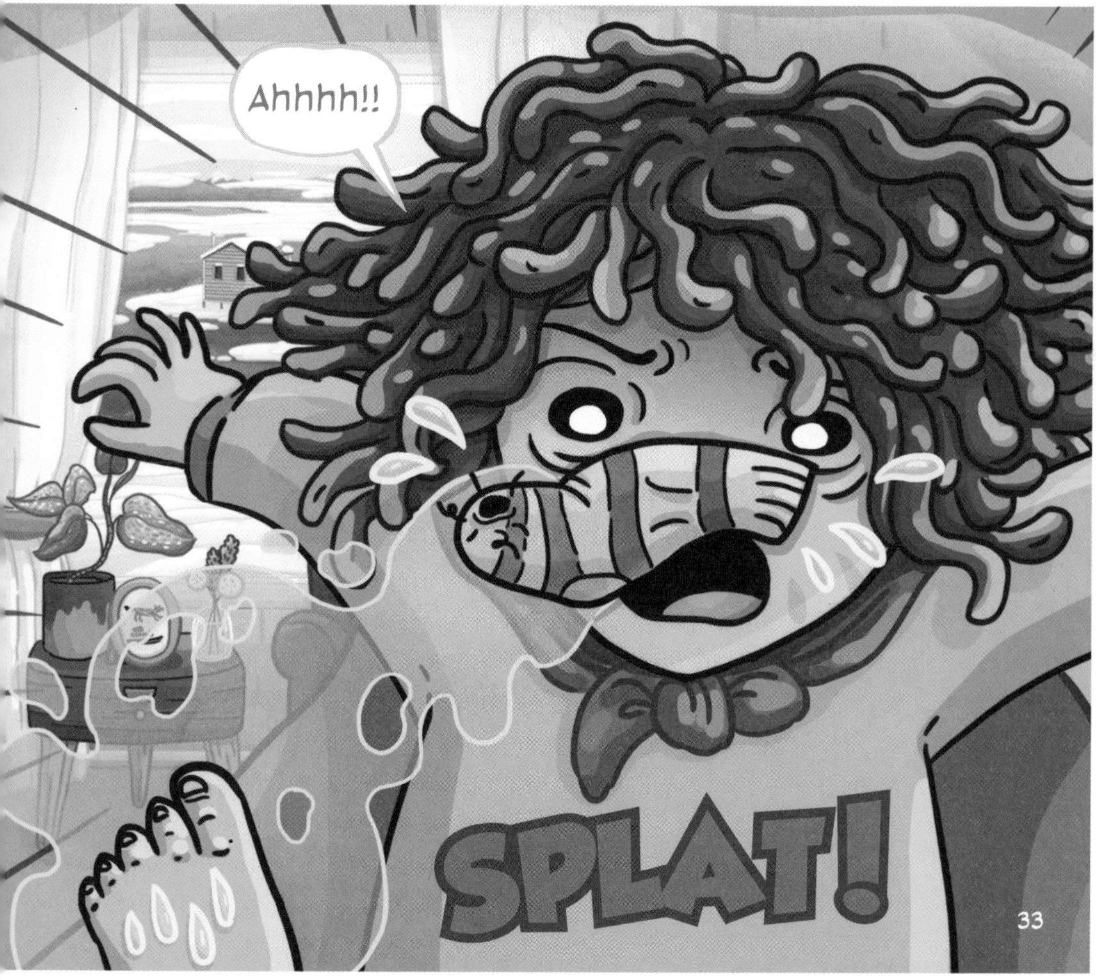
Ahhhh!!
SPLAT!

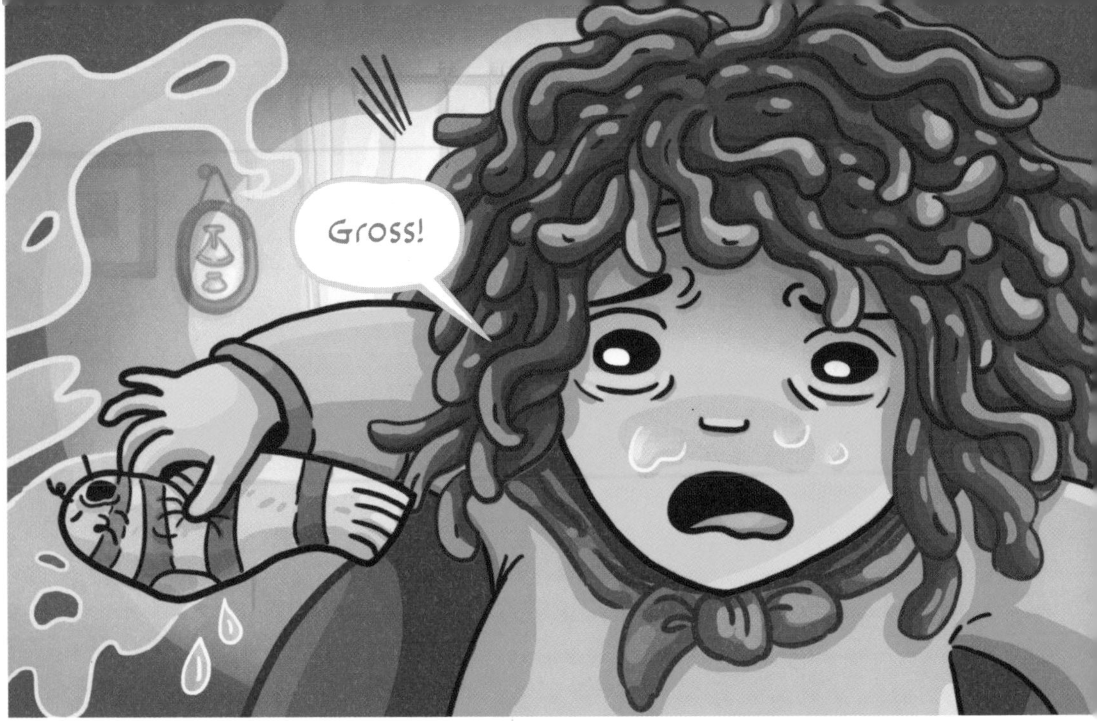
Gross!

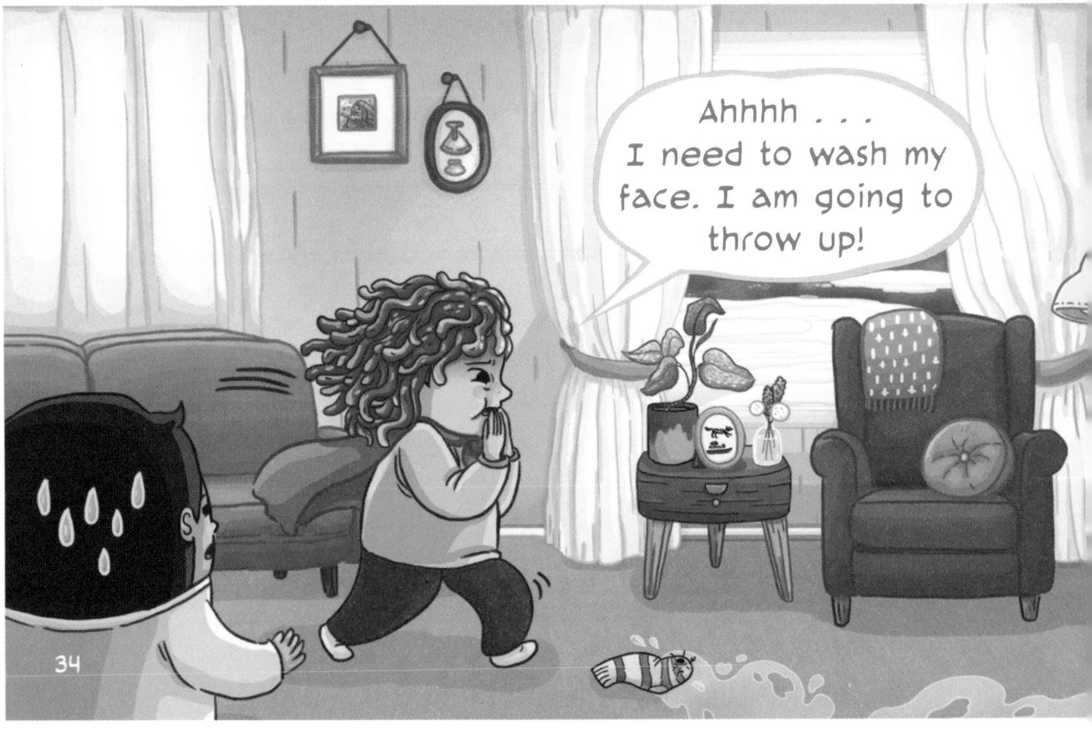
Ahhhh . . .
I need to wash my face. I am going to throw up!

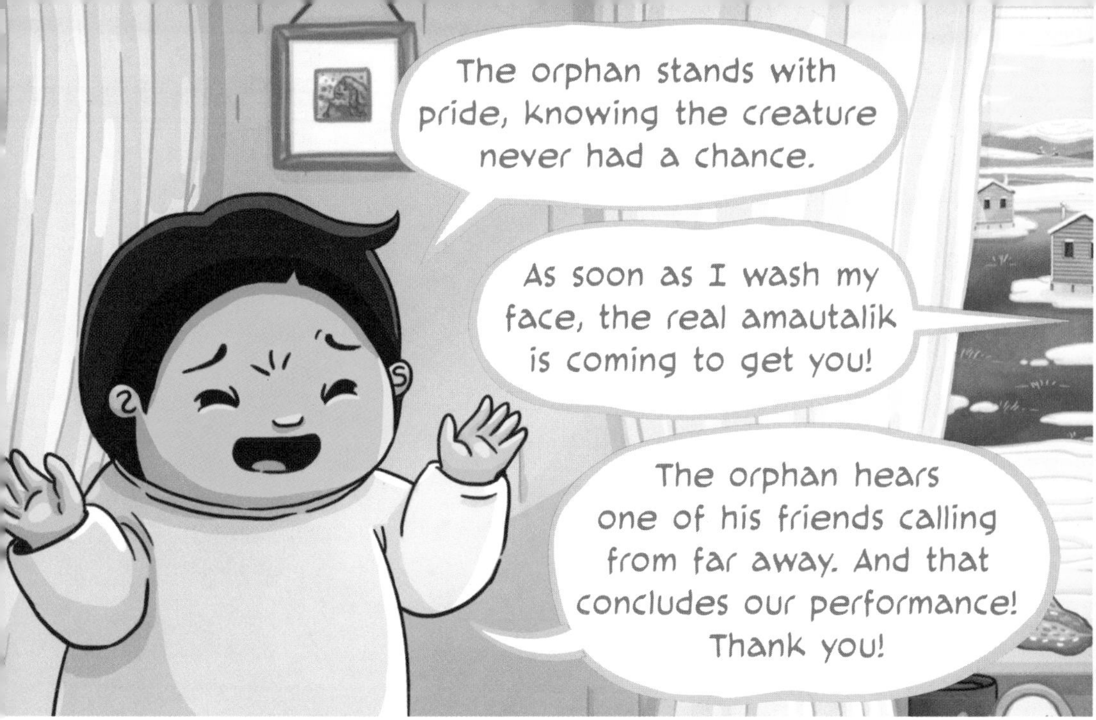
The orphan stands with pride, knowing the creature never had a chance.
As soon as I wash my face, the real amautalik is coming to get you!
The orphan hears one of his friends calling from far away. And that concludes our performance! Thank you!

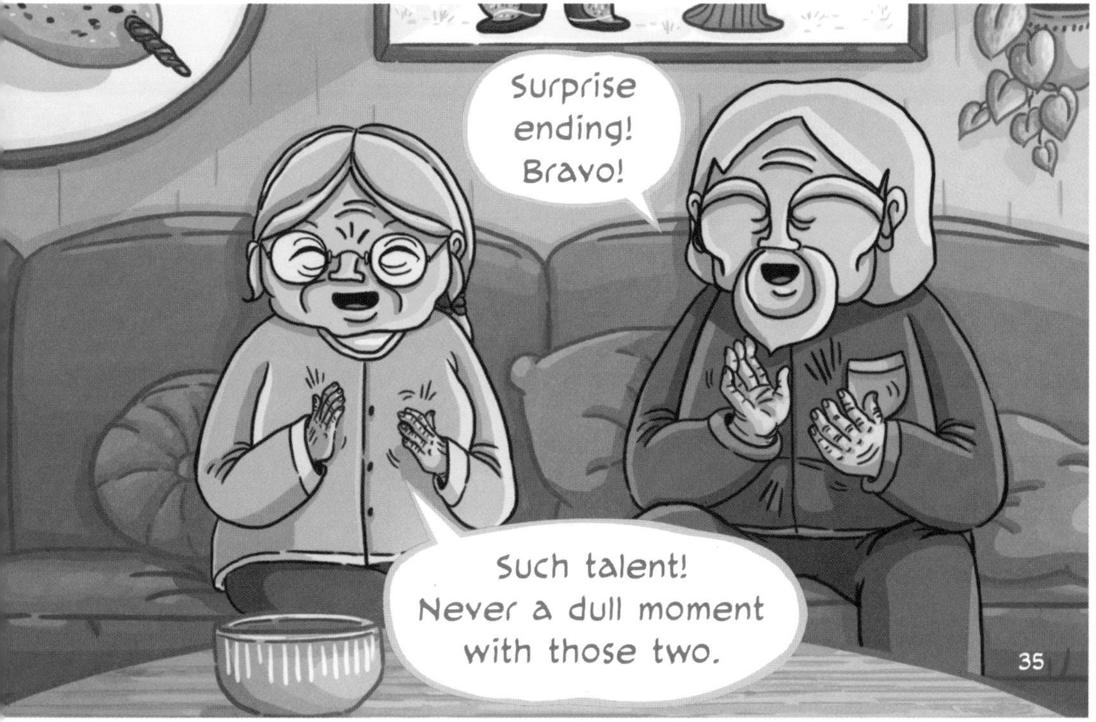
Surprise ending! Bravo!
Such talent! Never a dull moment with those two.

CONTRIBUTORS

Roselynn Akulukjuk was born in Pangnirtung, Nunavut, in the Canadian Arctic. In 2012, Roselynn moved to Toronto to pursue a career in film and attend the Toronto Film School, where she fell in love with being behind the camera. After finishing her studies and working in Toronto, Roselynn returned home to Nunavut, where she began working with Taqqut Productions, an Inuit-owned production company located in the capital of Nunavut, Iqaluit. Part of Roselynn's love of filmmaking is the ability to interview Elders, listen to their traditional stories, and share them with the world. In 2015, Roselynn wrote and directed her first film, the live-action and puppetry short *The Owl and the Lemming*, on which her book by the same title is based. Her film won Best Animation at the 2016 American Indian Film Festival.

Danny Christopher has travelled throughout the Canadian Arctic as an instructor for Nunavut Arctic College. He is the illustrator of *The Legend of the Fog*, *A Children's Guide to Arctic Birds*, and *Animals Illustrated: Polar Bear*. His work on *The Legend of the Fog* was nominated for the Amelia Frances Howard-Gibbon Illustration Award. He lives in Toronto with his wife, four children, and two bulldogs.

Astrid Arijanto spent her childhood drawing on any surface she could get her hands on, from papers to walls to all the white fences around her parents' house. Since then, her work has appeared in various media and publications across North America and Asia. She is the illustrator of *Putuguq and Kublu* and *Putuguq and Kublu and the Qalupalik!* She lives in Toronto and spends most of her days designing and illustrating beautiful books.

AMAUTALIIT

singular AMAUTALIK

The amautalik is an ogress from Inuit mythology that wanders the tundra in search of children. She has a basket made of driftwood on her back to carry away the children she finds wandering the land. She has long, unkempt hair and large, powerful hands. The basket on her back is very smelly, infested with bugs, and covered in slime to trap children inside.

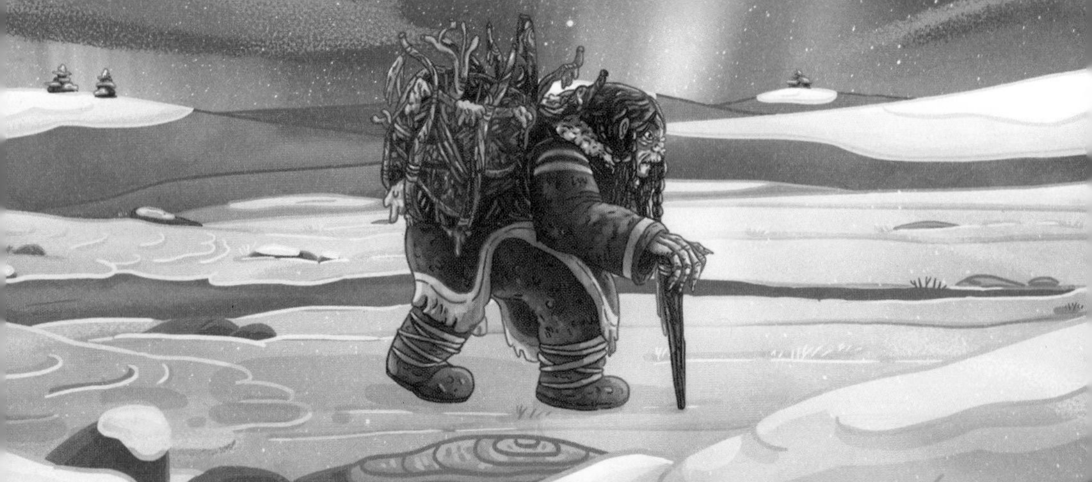

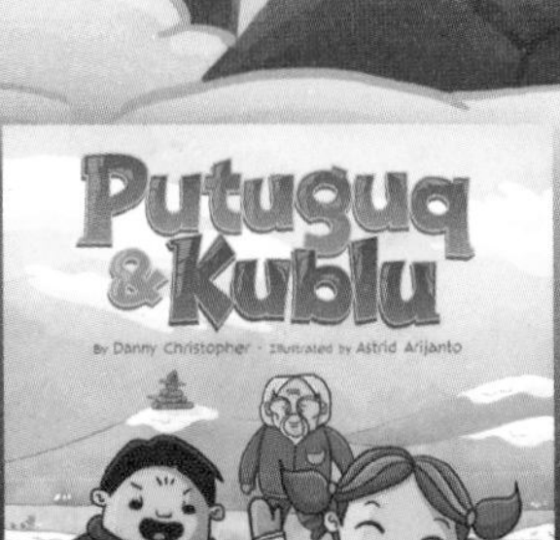
Putuguq & Kublu
By Danny Christopher · Illustrated by Astrid Arijanto

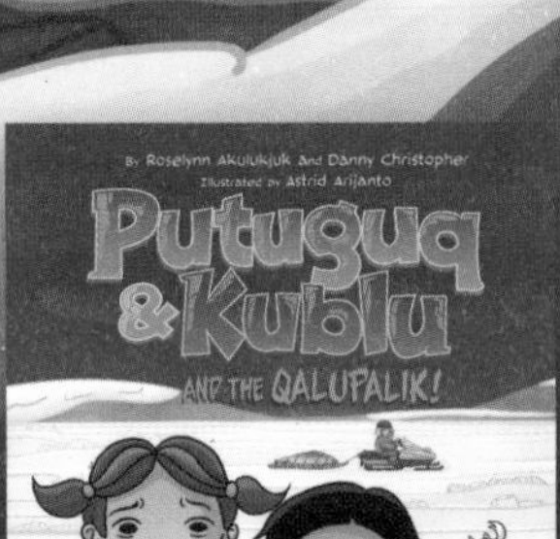
By Roselynn Akulukjuk and Danny Christopher
Illustrated by Astrid Arijanto
Putuguq & Kublu
AND THE QALUPALIK!

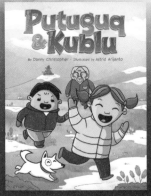

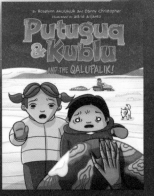